SPLITTING FIREWOOD

OTHER BOOKS BY DAVID TRESEMER:

**THE SCYTHE BOOK: Mowing Hay, Cutting Weeds,
and Harvesting Small Grains with
Hand Tools**

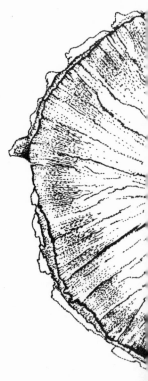

SPLITTING
FIREWOOD

by
David *Ward* Tresemer

*"Cleave the Wood
and there am I"*

Drawings by Tara Devereux

BY HAND & FOOT LTD. Brattleboro, Vermont
MCMLXXXI

LIBRARY OF CONGRESS CATALOGING IN PUBLICATION DATA

Tresemer, David Ward.
Splitting firewood.

Bibliography: p.
Includes index.
1. Fuelwood cutting. 2. Fuelwood cutting—
Folklore. I. Title.
SD536.5.T73   634.9'8   81-18124
ISBN 0-938670-01-8   AACR2

CREDITS

4: Pre-Columbian stone axes (Dumbarton Oaks, Washington, D.C.);

7: Ax handle of Abe Lincoln, New Salem, Illinois, 1834 (Photograph by Oliver Barrett, Frontispiece of first edition of *Abraham Lincoln: The Prairie Years* by Carl Sandburg);

10: Photograph by author;

19: Drawings by Aldren Watson;

20: After a figure by Rudolfs Drillis, in his "Folk Norms";

22: Ferdinand Hodler, 1910, "Der Holzfaller," 1910 (Kunstmuseum Bern, Bern, Germany);

23: From the fourteenth century "Miscellanea d'alchimia" (MS. Ashburnham 1166), Biblioteca Medicea-Laurenziana, Florence;

24: Detail from Claude-Joseph Vernet, *Le Matin* (courtesy of The Art Institute of Chicago);

25: From *History of Wood-Engraving* by George Woodberry;

26: After the photographs of slit gongs in John Layard's *Stone Men of Malekula*.

All the other figures were drawn by Tara Devereux.

Quotations from Ken Kesey's *Sometimes a Great Notion* courtesy of Viking Penguin Inc.; from Russel Lockhart's "Cancer in Myth and Dream" courtesy of Spring Publications of Dallas, Texas; from Helen Nearing's *Wise Words on the Good Life* courtesy of Helen Nearing; from John Wallace's *Conversations with Zackary Adams,* courtesy of Frederick Ungar of New York. Some portions of the section entitled, "Field Testing the Splitting Devices," appeared as a preliminary report of results in the September, 1980, issue of *Blair and Ketchum's Country Journal* (© September 1980 Country Journal Publishing Company, Inc. All rights reserved).

By Hand & Foot, Ltd.

Since 1976, By Hand & Foot, Ltd., has been engaged in an effort to import, manufacture, and improve the best in human-powered tools. We work with the following label:

Tools dependent on human energy.   ™
P. O. Box 611
Brattleboro, Vermont 05301

— integrated tool systems for kitchen, garden, and small farm

— for health, security, and independence

— tools which enhance rather than abuse our relationship to the task and to the earth

When comparing machine-powered and human-powered tools, our emphasis has been on replicable scientific experiments, that is, an objective analysis of the advantages and disadvantages of the different tools. However, we have not ignored subjective information from the human body, from emotional or spiritual experiences.

The results of our research are featured in a series of manuals on separate tools.

We feel it is very important to make available the tools discussed in each manual: all the tools described herein can be obtained from By Hand & Foot, Ltd.

Acknowledgments are due to Susan Tresemer for helping me to better understand The Wood, then to write about it; to Castle Freeman for editing the manuscript; to Bruce Hoadley, Larry Gay, Peter Payne, Bruce Cobbold, Stephen Bourne, David Buchdahl, and Bob Ames for reviewing parts of the manuscript; to Keith Squires, Stephen Bourne, and Sean McEntee for assisting in time trials; to Irving Perkins for carefully guiding the production of the printed work.

Preface

As man moves ever further from a genuine intimacy with nature and becomes ever more enmeshed in the frightening web of his own creation, the compensatory laws of psychic necessity bring forth individuals sensitive to the perils of the reality of this life in the modern world, and who in their own lives begin to stumble upon and are drawn into communion with the spirits of nature. Some can give voice to this new life, and for those with ears fortunate there can be a timely hearing of mankind's most urgent task—to reconnect his wandering and most troubled spirit with the ground of his being. That ground can be found in the most unlikely and neglected places, even in such a place and such an activity as splitting firewood. David Tresemer has been witness to the living spirit in the wood and in the act of splitting it. He prepares himself as for a solemn act and has attended to each detail of wood, ax, and axman, with a love and care that befits the sacred and ancient ritual of splitting one of nature's most remarkable gifts. In gentle words he conveys these subtle and too-long-forgotten things, in a work that becomes a song, a jubilus, that brings forth a celebration of those moments when man experiences not his mastery of nature but his communion with it. This is a wonderful book. As one who has only just moved from the city to the forest, this book excites deep yearnings in me to approach the trees and the harvest of firewood with a renewed sense of the profound meaning that lies beneath the surface of something that I had taken only for granted. And on top of this to have a kind of woodsplitter's almanac of vital and practical detail! What more could possibly be asked of such a little book! We people of the city would do well to come to know these fundamental experiences once again—to feel the ax in mother wood, to feel the warmth from logs of one's own cutting, to connect again to the mythic reality that wood excites. Can woodsplitting be a soulful experience? It seems so. Dr. Tresemer has shown us the way, but it must be *done*. A book cannot do that. Get your ax! Gather some wood! Experience the wonder of this!

Russell Lockhart

Contents

Contents

Foreword

OVER TWO thousand years ago, Plato said, "Field and forest will teach me nothing, but men do." This statement has apparently guided academic philosophy away from natural phenomena ever since the statement was made. My two books, *The Scythe Book: Mowing Hay, Cutting Weeds, and Harvesting Small Grains with Hand Tools* and *Splitting Firewood,* are my response to Plato's statement, quite naturally in disagreement.

SPLITTING
FIREWOOD

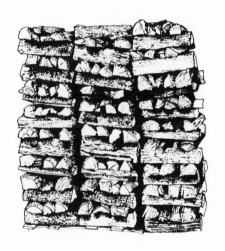

1. Why Split Wood?

But a blazing fire makes a house look more comely
upon a winter's day, when the son of Cronos sends
down snow.

> —Homer's Epigram XIII
> Seventh Century BC[1]

In the Western tradition, of which we are a part, the use of wood
for warmth goes back deep into history. Emerging from our
short-lived dependency on petroleum-derived energy we revive
the art of obtaining and preparing firewood. How different from
some early civilizations, typified by the seventeenth and eighteenth centuries in America, where huge trees were rolled into piles
and burned to remove their bulk from the place of intended
agriculture! How different from the overpopulated areas of today
where our ax is not known because there is no wood to cut![2]

Of the many tasks necessary to prepare trees for burning—
felling the tree, lopping off the branches, moving the log, bucking
the log to lengths, splitting the billets—the last is the most
frequently demanded of the fire builder. Even wood that is bought
from a wood dealer as "cut, split, and delivered," though it is cut to
length and delivered, is very seldom split into pieces of the right
size. For more efficient drying, more efficient burning, indeed
often just to fit through the door of the stove or furnace, com-
mercially split wood must usually be split further. Before the age
of coal at the beginning of the Industrial Revolution, standards
for the diameter or girth of firewood were fixed by law in Europe;
in other words, just *how* split split wood had to be was set by
statute. Now, in the absence of such standards, the commercial
wood dealer cannot afford the extra time to split wood into

1

smaller and smaller sticks. And yet, a billet two feet in diameter split into two, four, or even eight pieces is still too big for most space-heating or kitchen stoves. So every fire builder comes to the task of splitting.

TERMINOLOGY: FROM TREE TO FIRE

> Backlog and forestick were soon piled and kin-
> dlings laid.
> —Harriet Stone
> *Poganuc People,* 1878

Each form of wood in the progression from tree to fire has a distinct name. The *tree* is a "perennial plant with a single self-supporting woody stem growing to considerable size."[3] The trunk, bole, or stem of the tree is felled and shorn of its branches, and cut into eight- to sixteen-foot *logs.* The branches become either *topwood,* suitable for further bucking (crosscutting into sections), or they become *brushwood* or *slash,* usually too full of leaves and twigs to be sorted into firewood. A great deal of the mineral content of the tree is in the slash and bark, and it is good that the slash is usually left in the forest to feed future generations of trees. Small branches and some brushwood can be gathered and tied with a pliable willow shoot to become a *faggot.* The log is bucked up into pieces of the right length for burning, called *billets* (also sometimes *bolts*). The billets are split into *sticks.* Sticks are cleft wood instead of round wood; more surface area is exposed to the oxidation process of fire when billets are split, and thus the fire burns more actively. As William Austin concluded in 1622: "Surely many Sticks together, burne more vehemently than a single Billet."[4] Large oddly shaped pieces, such as the unsplit or partly split crotches of trees where branches meet, are called *chunks.* Every step with the saw produces *sawdust.* Every splitting or felling operation produces *chips* and *splinters,* which can be collected to help start the fire, and *kindling,* which are sticks split very small.

In the world of firewood the most precise terms are not always used, as when we say "throw another log on the fire"; or in the different usages of *stick:* "the carpenters were sent into the woods, to endeavor to find a stick proper for a foremast."[5] The terms *log, billet,* and *stick* are often used in place of each other; their etymological roots are relatively recent, unlike *tree, wood,* and *fire,* which can be traced back to the ancient Indo-European roots **deru-, widhu-,** and **pur-**.

The diagram in Figure 1 shows the different forms of wood in relationship to each other. The diagram is organized in terms of the dimension of heat; basically, every action we take uses up energy from a source other than the wood, making the heat finally harvested from the tree proportionately less useful. The grown tree represents a quantity of the sun's energy stored in the flesh of the plant. Though poised reaching up from the earth, it is shown in this picture at the bottom, located at its center of gravity. The stored energy seeks to ascend, to grow and interact with the sunlight. The minerals organized by this energy in the cellulose and lignin seek to descend, by the influence of gravity. When we harvest a tree and prepare it for burning, we contribute more energy or heat to the tree. We work our bodies and machines and/or animals. We also repeatedly lift the tree in its ever smaller pieces until we finally build the fire and set the match. At that point the flames rise up, the heat rises and radiates out and up, and the smoke lifts up the chimney. A small portion of the mass of the original tree (about one percent) settles into ash which we spread around our gardens and orchards where they are drawn again into the growth of plants. The energy or heat we use in every step literally and figuratively lifts the wood against gravity, making it less substantial and less economic as a source of heat.

Rudolf Steiner expresses it this way:

> The being of heat manifests exactly like the
> negation of gravity, like negative gravity.[6]

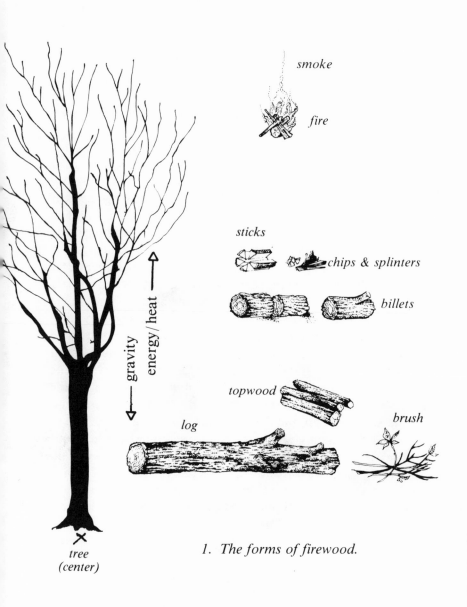

1. The forms of firewood.

There may, in fact, be a net energy loss when wood is harvested; that is, more energy may be consumed to harvest the wood than is released in its burning. Certainly this will be the case if we consider the energy lost through incomplete combustion of unseasoned wood, the energy lost through heat escaping up the flue of a poorly designed woodburning appliance, and the energy lost through inefficiency in design and use of harvesting tools.

THE CORD

A special set of terms is used to describe quantities of firewood. Our *cord,* so-called because it was once measured with a cord, contains 128 cubic feet, a stack four feet high, four feet deep, and eight feet long. A French cord in Quebec is eight feet, six inches, by four feet, by four feet, three inches—or 144 cubic feet. The British *stack* is 108 cubic feet. A *load* is six-and-a-quarter cords, or 800 cubic feet. A *sloop* is a boat-full of firewood, usually thirty cords.

A *rick* or *face cord* is also four feet high and eight feet long, but it is only twelve to twenty-four inches deep. The ruse of delivering a face cord to an unwary urbanite or out-of-towner while charging him for a full cord had become common enough for the Commonwealth of Massachusetts to prohibit recently the use of the term *cord* in sales of firewood, substituting the word *unit* to mean 128 cubic feet.

It has often been suggested that firewood should be sold by weight, since measurements have shown that the actual volume of solid fuel in a cord varies between 58 and 100 cubic feet. These measurements were made in piles carefully stacked by forestry researchers, and do not indicate the favorite method used by wood dealers through history to increase the amount of space occupied by a fixed amount of wood. A story from Maine illustrates the art of deceitful wood stacking:

> Skin Jubb landed a load of cordwood at Jim's store
> a few weeks ago, small stuff, and half of it crook-

edr'n a dog's hind leg. Skin took his pay and started
to hurry off as Jim went out to look it over. But 'fore
Skin got out of hearin' Jim called him back—then
handed him a quarter extry and a fi'cent cigar.
"Wut's all this for?" says Skin.

"Waal," says Jim, "the quarter is for the extry time
you must-a spent huntin' up the smallest, crookedest
sticks you could find—and the cigar's a prize for
stackin' 'em up into a cord o' wood you could chase a
cat through from any p'int of the compass!"[7]

Compare a line from Philip Massinger's comedy of 1632, "The
City Madame" (Act II, scene 1):

Though the dishes were raised one upon another
As woodmongers do billets.

One proposal to standardize the quantity of wood being
measured has been that every log be scaled to determine the
volume of solid wood it contained. Then sales would be by the
"c-unit," equalling 100 cubic feet of solid wood no matter how
much space it takes up. This idea requires simply a log rule and
lots of paper for calculations; but it would be very difficult for a
wood dealer to keep track of all the measured piles of wood, and
many of the crooked trees culled for firewood elude accurate
measurement.

Even careful stacking gives different quantities of wood in
cords made up of different sizes of wood. One measurement
study found that a cord of logs of very large diameter (average
fifteen inches, or thirty logs of four-foot-long wood per cord) or
very small diameter (average six inches, or 150 logs per cord)
have less solid wood content than logs with diameters between
eight and ten inches (and seventy to ninety logs per cord). The
intermediate logs had 82.7 cubic feet of solid wood per cord,
whereas the small and the large logs had around seventy-four
cubic feet per cord, a loss of over ten percent. Another study
found fifty-eight cubic feet of solid wood in a cord of unpeeled
hardwood tops six inches in diameter and four feet long, compared to ninety-eight cubic feet in a cord of smooth and straight

hardwood logs twelve inches in diameter and four feet long (a loss of forty percent).

In another measurement study, a cord of stacked wood of different sorts was thrown into a five-foot-square bin, much as it would be by a wood dealer. When the length of each billet was twelve inches and the wood was round or unsplit, the volume of the helter-skelter pile was 140 cubic feet; when the wood was cleft, 155 cubic feet; when the wood was a mixture of round and cleft, 145 cubic feet. With billets sixteen inches long and unsplit, the cord became 155 cubic feet, mixed round and cleft, 160 cubic feet.[8]

On the basis of these studies it seems possible to guess at the quantity of solid wood in a pile if the length of the billets and the girth of the sticks are known.

GIRTH

The size into which wood should be split, so as to be durable in burning, and yet give sufficient heat, is a matter worthy of some consideration. If split very small, any given quantity will give more heat for a while, but will be quickly consumed; if large, it will consume slowly, but will burn less readily, and give much less heat.

—*American Mechanics' Magazine*
August 27, 1825

Assessing the girth of firewood has special importance—the smaller the girth, the greater the surface area per volume of a stick, and thus the quicker the fire that the wood will make. Special terms were once used to describe what sort of wood was in a fixed volume of measure, terms that referred specifically to the girth of the split wood. *Faggot, talwood,* and *talshides* were categories of firewood defined by royal decrees of Edward VI and Elizabeth I in sixteenth-century England. *Fascines, coppicewood, driftwood, windfalls, dotterels,* and *wastewood* were other delightful terms used in Great Britain and America to describe specific sorts of wood of small girth.

The most complete definitions of types of firewood can be found in a German forestry text from 1894, giving fourteen main classes:

1. *Split billets,* thoroughly sound wood, subdivided into two classes according to size.
2. *Crooked billets,* sound but knotty.
3. *Broken wood.* Unsound split billets subdivided into two classes according to degree of unsoundness.
4. *Round billets* from stems.
5. *Round billets* from branches.
6. *Peeled round billets* from oak-coppice where the bark is used for tanning.
7. *Root-wood.* This may be divided into two classes when it sells well.
8. *Large unsplit pieces* (chunks).
9. *Small split billets* fastened with willow withes.
10. *Faggots* without twigs of larger wood from thinnings under 2½ inches in diameter.
11. *Branch-faggots.*
12. *Faggots of thorns,* etc., from hedge trimmings.
13. *Heaped-up faggot wood* (not bound with withes).
14. *Bark* for fuel, often rolled.[9]

While most firewood quantity and quality standards in the United States have been informal agreements between individual buyers and sellers, the Commissioner of Agriculture for the state of Connecticut in 1933 specified three classes of firewood, depending on girth:

1. *Fireplace wood.* Fancy grade, to include hickory and white oak. Grade A, to include all the oaks, black, yellow and paper birch, beech, ash and sugar maple. Requirements: clean, straight, uniform in size, free from rot and holes, seasoned, pieces 4 inches to 8 inches in diameter, all over 5 inches to be split.
2. *Furnace wood.* Fancy grade to include all oaks, hickory, black birch, sugar maple and ash. Grade A, to include above species and red maple. Requirements: same as fireplace wood, except larger than 8 inches to be split.
3. *Range (or stove) wood.* Fancy grade, to include any of the woods

listed in fancy fireplace and furnace woods. Grade A, to include any of the woods listed above. Requirements: same as for above grades except for size; pieces to be 2 inches to 4 inches round or split, all over 4 inches to be split.

The application of these standards to the task of splitting is suggested in Figure 2. The definitions from the Connecticut classification scheme are used to show how much splitting need be done to produce similar burning sticks from different diameter billets. It is meant only as a general guideline since few billets are perfect geometric shapes, nor can we easily split a billet

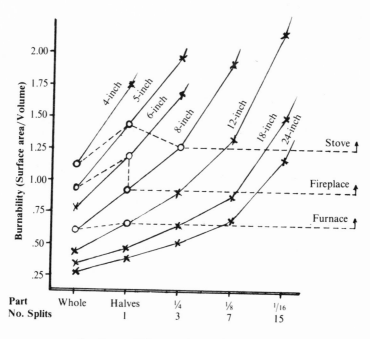

2. Burnability and number of splits.

twelve to twenty-four inches in diameter into sixteen identical pieces. The size and shape of spaces between the surfaces of wood are quite important, so setting sticks in a stove closely or far apart also makes a great difference in their burnability. This graph assumes that the wood is stacked in the stove in the same sort of way, that the cubic feet of air per minute passing through the stove is the same, that the wood has a uniformly low moisture content, and so forth. The laboratories which measure wood-burning performance of different appliances end up with extremely complicated formulas and many arbitrary assumptions about these conditions of burning. Conditions vary from one fire to the next, but this graph is valuable in showing how the wood is changed by splitting to make it potentially more burnable.

It would not be difficult to bring back simple standards of girth in firewood, and adjust costs accordingly. Figure 3 shows a girth measurement device: a piece of plywood with four holes, four, six, eight, and ten inches in diameter. Piled up behind this measuring device are sticks that have fit through the holes, with, from left to right, the four-inch sticks, then six-inch, eight-inch, ten-inch, and the pieces that would not fit.

The main criticism of this wood-sizing device is that sticks are seldom round, but more often triangular and oddly shaped. They don't slip neatly through circular holes. Yet fitting sticks through circular holes seems far more practical than measuring the perimeter of each stick with a tape measure. The ratios of surface area to volume for circles and triangles are very similar through a range of dimensions, the differences becoming inconsequential in the normal variations of the woodpile. Given the variation in shapes of sticks, this girth-measurer is accurate enough to differentiate between one woodpile and another.

Having experimented with simple girth standards for my own wood, I find myself in agreement with the Connecticut classifications. The smallest sticks, with an outside diameter of four inches or less, are what I would prefer for a cookstove; six inches

3. Sorting sticks by their girth.

or less are for the fireplace, with a few eight-inch pieces for the "backlog"; and eight- and ten-inch billets split once are suitable for most furnaces, with occasional chunks for holding the fire overnight. In a pile of sticks of different girths, a small portion of the pile could be measured with a device like the one pictured, the relative amounts of the different girths in the pile compared, and the price for the pile adjusted accordingly. The smaller-girth wood would command the greater price.

At present, few loads of delivered firewood would qualify for any of the old Connecticut classes, and the Department of

Agriculture in Connecticut has forgotten that the regulations ever existed. I traveled to two different cordwood salesmen, and sized samples of their firewood; forty percent by volume were eight-inch sticks, forty percent were ten-inch sticks, and the remaining twenty percent were divided in volume between six-inch and over ten-inch sticks. You can't rely on wood suppliers to give you wood of the girths you need. It is the fire maker's task to prepare the fuel properly. Whether you fell the tree or not, you must split your firewood.

2. The Tools To Use

The French philosopher Jean Jacques Rousseau once lamented
our dependence on tools:

> The body of a savage man being the only instrument
> he understands, he uses it for various purposes, of
> which ours, for want of practice, are incapa-
> ble. . . . If he had had an axe, would he have been
> able with his naked arm to break so large a branch
> from a tree?[1]

Preparing wood for burning in any great quantity with the bare
hands is beyond our present capabilities, and we must choose a
tool to help us.

THE AX

Crude stone axes have been in the hands of humans for hundreds
of thousands of years. Elegant stone axes, with sharp edges and
helves of wood, were the development of the Neolithic ("new
stone") Revolution, the bridge from savagery to civilization.
Neolithic men settled down from a nomadic existence to become
food-growers instead of food-foragers, animal husbandmen
instead of hunters. Open spaces were needed for their planned
agricultural economy. The stone ax was used for the clearing, and
also for the cultivation, of cropland ten thousand years ago.

Improvements in the shape, material, and method of manufacture of stone axes were pre-historical; we do not have a record of
these developments as we do in the case of other tools, such as the
scythe. Yet we need only look at the implements of any stone age
culture to see the profusion and diversity of axes, and to guess at

their importance to and magical meaning in the lives of earlier men. Figure 4 illustrates how the work of axes became associated with energies within the tool, and came to have a ceremonial significance for the culture. The ornaments on these axes from Costa Rica, which seem so fierce, can be matched by axes from many cultures. They suggest the feeling necessary to approach the giant trees in a climax forest in order to bring them down. These images also suggest the function for which the ax was most highly praised though least used: warfare and execution. The same association of ax with destruction exists to the present day, as in the reference in *Alice's Adventures in Wonderland:* "Talking of axes," said the Duchess, "chop off her head!"

The ax was seen as a weapon of the gods, a symbol of lightning and thunder, since the first axes, called "thunderstones," were flung down by the gods to split whole trees.[2] The ax was also a symbol of the sun, a clever cleaver of the way, and a teacher of perseverance in overcoming obstacles. The uniformity of design and significance across all cultures is a very powerful statement of the ax's meaning in relationship to men.

Early metal axes were worked into the shape of their stone predecessors, since the metals were considered to be unripe stones. By working on them, the smiths ripened them, making them good stones. Metal axes were also highly ornamented, though more abstractly than stone axes. With mass production the reverence for and the ornament of axes have ceased, but the reasons for the esteem of the ax can be experienced by anyone who spends a day using one.

The single tool most frequently used for working wood in all its forms was and is the ax, as witness the following typical accounts. The first account is about North America after discovery by Columbus:

> With the crooked knife and the ax, the Indian or
> Eskimo can accomplish wonders in any woodwork-
> ing. Canoes, paddles, ax and adz handles, wooden
> spoons, wooden bowls, drinking cups, snowshoe

4. *Stone axes from Costa Rica.*

frames, etc., are produced with a skill that rivals the
work of the white craftsman equipped with the very
best of modern tools.

The second account is about two cousins homesteading in Hard-
wick, Vermont, in the summer of 1793:

They had no such thing as a team or even a hoe to
work with; but with their axes they hewed out
wooden hoe blades from maple chips, hardened them
in the fire, and took saplings for handles. With these
they hoed in two acres of wheat.[3]

Axes have in the past been made in many different styles and
weights depending on the tradition in which they were made and
the task for which they were needed. The European axes were
heavier in weight than our modern felling ax. The so-called
"American" ax was lighter and better balanced, with a poll on the
side of the head opposite the edge. With this counterbalance, the
handle did not require such a firm grip to keep the blade from
deviating from its intended direction when struck horizontally.
This style of ax was widely used in this country beginning in the
eighteenth century. With it a man could fell three times as many
trees as with its English counterpart.[4] It is, however, difficult to
accept the historians' conclusion that the polled ax was original to
America after seeing several polled axes in William Petrie's *Tools
and Weapons*—including an ax nearly identical to the splitting ax
of today that was dug up from ancient Nineveh.

All axes have a convex bevel at the cutting edge, but just how fat
the steel becomes behind the edge—its degree of "wedge"—makes
a great difference in its function. Axes were once named wedge,
half-wedge, and quarter-wedge. The wedge ax was the thickest,
and was used for splitting billets or logs, the half wedge for cutting
the limbs off a felled tree, and the quarter-wedge for chopping.
The double-bitted ax usually carried a sharp and thin quarter-
wedge on one side for felling and a thicker edge on the other side
for rougher work. Old felling axes, ground and reground in the
process of sharpening, so that the area behind the edge had more

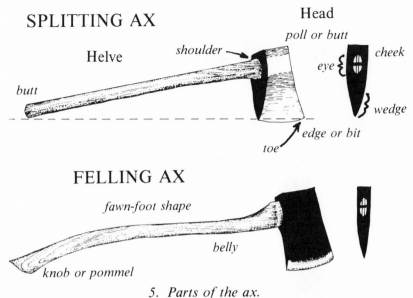

SPLITTING AX

Head

poll or butt

Helve

shoulder

butt

eye

cheek

wedge

edge or bit

toe

FELLING AX

fawn-foot shape

belly

knob or pommel

5. Parts of the ax.

wedge to it, became splitting axes. The *Holzaxt* brought by Germans to Pennsylvania was particularly fat behind the edge and might be called a double-wedge; its function was to split wood.

Examples of traditional European splitting axes shown in Figure 6 all lack the poll that we associate with the ax. Yet in a vertical movement such as splitting, a poll is not needed to balance the weight on the helve, and in fact could tend to twist the ax when the wood is struck. The poll has ironically become traditional, though it is not really needed in this application.

The old stone axes were by necessity fairly thick and were used more like splitting axes than felling axes; when bringing down a tree, the stroke was at a steep angle to the line of cut, and the kerf was very broad. In some cases these axes are more effective than the American felling ax; in a tree-cutting contest in Borneo in Indonesia in 1926, the workers with the quarter-wedge ax lost to natives skilled in the use of their stone axes.[5]

Splitting axes today look very much like the German *Holzaxt*. They are occasionally called splitting mauls, but the meaning of

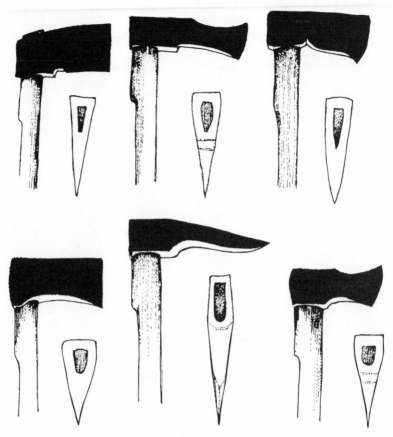

6. Some traditional splitting axes of Europe.

maul is to crush or grind. Though heavier than a felling ax, splitting axes certainly do not crush the wood, and therefore they are not properly called mauls.

MANUFACTURE

I would like to summarize the steps of manufacture of the ax to show to what degree its essence is concentrated heat, or sun's energy, an observation important later on (see especially Chapter 5).

Iron ore is mined if the concentration of iron oxide in the soil is greater than twenty-five percent. At the mine, the ore is crushed, and combed with a magnet to leave behind the low-grade tailings, refining the ore to sixty percent iron. Bentonite clay is added to hold the iron particles together in pellet form. The pellets are baked in an oven to strengthen them against crumbling during transit to the blast furnace. The blast furnace, or smelter, is a steel shell over a hundred feet high, lined with firebrick. Once hot, it is not allowed to cool until the firebrick needs replacement. The pellets are mixed at the top with limestone and coke (a high-quality coal which has been baked to drive off volatile gases). At the bottom, air and gases heated to 1,700 degrees are blown into the furnace. As they roar upwards, the hot gases meet the concentrated coal; the temperatures created by this intense chemical reaction melt the iron out of the pellets. The molten iron gathers in a pool at the base of the furnace, impurities or slag floating on the top. The molten iron is drawn from the bottom and poured into molds to form "pigs."

The cooled pigs are then sent to the steel mill, where they are melted and poured into large vats narrow at the top. A huge hollow needle is inserted into the center of the vat through which oxygen is bubbled at high pressures. The oxygen combines with any remaining carbon in the molten iron to make carbon dioxide gas, and the bubbling continues until the carbon content is below 1.5 percent. Low-carbon steels (under .25 percent C) are used for rivets and nails; medium-carbon steels (.25–.55 percent) for gears and axles; high-carbon steels (over .55 percent) for hammers, axes, and chisels; and very high-carbon steels (over .9 percent) for drills and files. Traces of other elements are added at this stage of steel manufacture to make the particular sort of steel required; for example, the steel used for splitting axes has traces of manganese, phosphorus, and sulphur.

The molten steel is cooled and formed into standard shapes such as bars and rounds. At the forge, the round stock (2¼ inches for splitting axes) is sawn into lengths called billets (!), which are then set into a furnace until they glow bright yellow. Held with long tongs, a billet is placed onto the open mold (die) in the hammer press. A weight of 3,500 pounds is released, falls several feet to hit the hot metal with a kinetic energy of 15,000 foot-pounds, is lifted quickly by a system of large turning wheels and belts, is released again. Five strikes are usually adequate to mold the steel into the shape of an ax, with some extra metal extruded around the sides. This extra (called "flash") is cut away in another machine. The ax head is then set into an extremely powerful hydraulic press, which pushes out a part of the steel to make the ax eye. Before this machine was used, an eye was formed by bending a flat bar of softer steel into a U-shape, then welding the ends together, with a piece of harder steel in between for a bit. The opening at the base of the closed U became the eye of the ax.

The forged ax head cools in a bin, then is ground on a high-speed wheel-shaped stone. All felling axes, and some splitting axes, are then hardened by heating the cutting edge over a flame. When the edge glows orange, the hot ax head is plunged into heavy brine (water would explode), then baked in a tempering oven. The temperature of the oven, the amount of time at that temperature, and the rapidity of cooling, all affect the crystalline structure of the steel, and thus its behavior when in use.[6]

I have observed the smelting described here in different places at different times. I have observed the forging in the shop of a small smithy as well as in the factory. Both are filled with noise and heat, with fumes, smoke, and steam intermingling beneath the blackened roof to obscure the sight of anything but the glowing fire and metal. This is the domain of Hephaistos, Greek god of the forge and the smith. The noise of the hammer on anvil is loud, but the noise of the 3,500-pound press is deafening. The machine must be set upon a foundation of concrete and steel weighing thirty-five tons to keep it from destroying itself.

In earlier times the furnace was tended by hand, and the ax

beaten between a hammer and an anvil. There was less understanding of the molecular structure of metals, and a great deal less mechanization in the making of the ax. Many magical notions grew up around the processes of smelting and forging, and specific rituals were observed at each step, some of which had the desired effect on the metal and which seem to us extraneous. All the rituals were justified, however, by a unified conception of the sacred nature of the art of smithing. The most common conception was that Mother Nature was gestating these metals, which would in time become more perfect; the smith was hurrying this process. Through his sacred art, the primal force has been aroused and matured in the ax. After a time of use and care, the primal force intermingles with the user and the ax becomes personalized. Thus, one's ax is not loaned. This tradition is found in lumbering camps still within the memory of some, as well as in primitive cultures where the ax is buried with its owner when he dies.[7]

With modern methods of steel-making, the exactitude of the smelting and forging permits a wider range of applications and a more durable product. The modern ax, however, has not been closely handled by a master smith. Its essential power has not been awakened. Judging from the adventures featured at the cinema, this power is what is sought—a metal implement charged with God's energy. Whether understood in a metaphorical or in a real way, the modern ax improves with use and care (discussed especially in Chapter 4).

Some splitting axes are cheaply produced by casting the steel in molds. But as the metal cools, the molecules do not align themselves in any particular way, pointing in every direction; these axes are very prone to chipping on impact. The cast head can sometimes be spotted by the burr of metal along the seam between the two casting molds, or by the pimple-like casting marks on the surface, or by a thick coat of paint applied to hide these defects.

The better splitting axes are drop-forged, in the mighty pro-

cess described above. The working of the metal aligns the molecules in a single direction, and strain-hardens the entire piece,
giving the whole a desirable strength and integrity. The drop-
forged head is usually bright and shiny, and, when tapped, has a
"ring" to it like a bell.

THE HELVE

> A stiff handle will make you awful lame if you use it a
> lot, make your shoulders ache—just ache all over—
> and it's only because your ax handle is stiff—there's
> no give to it. Where you buy a good, handmade
> handle, and it whips, you know, you might say [it is]
> limber, and it doesn't lame you . . . some like a
> twenty-eight inch; some like a thirty-two; some like
> even up to a thirty-six.
>   —Leo Merril, Passadumkeag, Maine[8]

The ax helve (or "haft" or "handle") improved upon handheld
stones by increasing the leverage, power, and range of the tool
while decreasing the recoil of the strike. A great deal of attention
was given by early artisans to the material and shape of the
handle. Sapwood and not heartwood was preferred because it
is more elastic and tenacious. The root end of the tree, considered to be toughest, was connected to the ax head because the
major stress on the handle is there. Faster growing trees, with
fewer growth rings to the inch, were considered superior. In
hickory, seventeen rings per inch was considered the maximum
number for the best wood, in ash, ten rings per inch.

Each woodsman, through trial and error in the whittling of
helves, found a shape that suited his or her style best, and kept a
pattern of this shape to guide the making of replacements. For
felling, some sort of knob was desirable at the end of the helve to
prevent the ax from sliding out of the hand, and many preferred a
gentle curve along the helve's length. The result was the "fawn-

foot" shape (seen in Figure 5 and on the Chopper 1 in Figure 9). The range of movements required for splitting firewood is not as great as for felling, so the helve for the splitting ax traditionally took on a straight shape without a knob at the butt.

As we shall see in the section on modern splitting tools, helves are made of several materials, including wood, steel, fiberglass, and new types of plastic-coated fiberglass. Comparing the performances of the different splitting devices makes it very clear what one wants in a handle. The length of the handle is needed to accelerate the ax head to deliver a blow greater by many times than could be achieved by the simple weight of the head alone. For greatest efficiency, the weight and length of the helve must vary according to the weight of the ax head. In Latvia, the length of the helve in a felling ax was traditionally twenty-four inches when the weight of the head was three pounds. But when the ax was for splitting, with an ax head that weighed seven pounds, a longer helve was required, traditionally the length of the user's arm. The greater efficiency of a light and long helve for a heavier ax head is confirmed by mathematical analysis of the vectors of force in the splitting stroke.[9]

The helve must be firm but not stiff in order to absorb the vibration of impact without jarring the hands and arms; that is, it must have *resilience,* defined as "the amount of strain energy which can be stored in a structure without causing permanent damage to it."[10] It is this ability to soak up sudden shocks without passing them on that is valuable. Steel pipe, as used in the Monster Maul (Figure 9), has very little resilience. Fiberglass has somewhat less resilience than wood. Wood has the most spring, and is the most comfortable to use. I suspect the makers of the new fiberglass handles know this, since they disguise their helves to look like wood.

"But," one protests who has read the advertisements for steel and fiberglass, "wood breaks!" Yes, after splitting a few cords, I fully expect to break an unprotected ax handle due to mistaken aim when I am tired. But, first, good technique prevents breaking helves. Second, I do not think a fiberglass handle would help this situation. I know how a wood helve acts when it is breaking, and I can act appropriately in response to how far the handle is gone. I do not know how fiberglass acts upon breaking, and fiberglass handles *will break.*

An unconditional replacement guarantee for broken fiberglass handle is no help for three reasons:

1.) the broken handle is extremely difficult to remove from the eye of the head—it must first be chipped out with a drill and the last of the epoxy cement must be burned out;

2.) I lose time awaiting the replacement; and

3.) while I am using the ruptured fiberglass handle, I am exposed to the frayed ends of thousands of broken glass filaments. I am acquainted with several people who have cut their hands on these needles of glass. Most fiberglass handles supposedly protect one from such an injury by attaching a rubber grip to the last eight inches of the helve, but restricting the hands to this area only prevents any sort of powerful stroke.

Some fiberglass handles are advertised as "indestrubctible," but I do not think this is possible. It just takes longer to bang up a fiberglass handle. Furthermore, the "indestructible" label encourages a more careless approach which can lead to splitting accidents. I prefer to carry the attitude of the old woodsman who bragged he had used the same ax for fifty years. "Really?" inquired the listener. "Yep," said the woodsman, "And it's had five new handles and two new heads."

To make a replacement helve for a splitting ax, locate a straight-grain log of the appropriate length—twenty-eight to thirty-six inches—and species—ash, oak, hickory, and horn-beam have superior resilience. With a froe and a mallet (Figures 13 and 14), rive a section of sapwood along the grain. Shape this section with a drawshave, holding it in a shaving horse, vise, or ax-handle brake. Most "store-bought" helves have greater girth than they need, probably as insurance against defects in the wood or accidental cutting across the grain. When you rive out your own helve, and have full advantage of straight grain, you can slim the handle to give a delightful spring unknown in any medium but wood. There must be a rise in the wood below where the helve fits the eye to hold the head in place. Finish by sanding with sandpaper or scraping with a piece of broken glass until smooth. Wipe the helve with several coats of a penetrating oil to seal the wood's pores against moisture: a mixture of linseed oil and turpentine is traditional, but newer, lighter oils exclude moisture more effectively and do not get sticky in warm weather. Some woodsmen touch the surface of a new helve with a flame to cauterize the wood cells and thus close off the access to moisture. The early-wood (spring growth) of the grain darkens more readily in the flame than the latewood and leaves an interesting pattern. Finally, the end of the helve must be sawn to make room for the helve wedge. Drew Langsner's *Country Woodcraft* illustrates several of these steps with pictures.

To hang the ax, lightly soap or grease the ax eye and tap the new helve in as far as it will go. Saw off any wood protruding beyond the ax head. When laid on the floor, as in Figure 5, the bit should rest on the floor near the center of its edge. If it does not, the helve that fits in the eye must be carefully whittled until the ax lies right in this test. Holding the ax vertically, tap the butt of the helve on the ground until the head is firmly in place. Finally, hammer in a wood or steel helve-wedge or both to hold the ax head in place.

A test of good hafting developed by the Intermediate Technology Development Group in Great Britain is to clamp the ax head in a vise with blocks of wood placed so that the head will not move while a weight of a hundred pounds is tied to the butt end. If after two minutes there is no permanent damage and no bend of the butt of the helve in excess of 25 mm from the original position, the ax is ready to be used.[11]

A helve connection is basically a mortise-and-tenon joint, and suffers from the same problems that those joints do when the relative humidity of the atmosphere changes from one season to another. Worse, the mortise in this case does not move a little when the tenon is swelled with moisture as does a mortise of wood. The result is crushed fibers in the helve which, when the wood is drier as in winter, shrink to make a loose fitting. Thus the superstition: "Don't leave an ax sticking in a live tree or chopping block at night; your body would ache and pain and spoil your rest." A well-oiled helve, covered in plastic in a dry shed when not in use, is the best prevention.

If you are unable to make your own ax helve, then content yourself with a store-bought replacement helve. Beware of helves which are cleverly painted with brown and white paint to simulate straight grain. Let the notion of different feels in different helves to tantalize you into learning how to use these tools. Figure 7 shows one of Abraham Lincoln's ax helves, with his name and the date carved upon it. Lincoln was a successful cordwood dealer in his youth; his helve shows some of the liberties one can take in the design of the ax helve. Even a store-bought helve can be modified to your liking with careful use of a sharp drawshave and scraper.

Clearly a lot of fuss went into making a helve, described well in Robert Frost's "The Ax-Helve." The helve was the wood that connected the chopper to the "thunderstone," and thence to the wood again. It was a very personal thing, and among some lumbermen the superstition grew that if you dropped your ax and someone else picked it up, or if someone else borrowed your ax, you would have to change the helve.[12]

FIELD TESTING THE MODERN SPLITTING DEVICES

What is the best way to split wood? Competing claims abound in advertisements found in nearly every magazine, all claiming greater efficiency of time and effort. Some salesmen give specific

7. Abe Lincoln's helve.

figures to support their point; for example, "user can split and stack up to a cord of wood an hour." My neighbor tells me he split seven cords in a day with a rented hydraulic splitter . . . with two friends. Then I read, "Man beats machine! Monster Maul defeats 'world's best' power log splitter in competition." Monster Maul?

To determine what might be the best splitting technique for the owner of a wood cookstove or small to mid-range space-heating stove, I set out to compare the available techniques in a woodsplitting experiment. I obtained over thirty of the most popular and most advertised power and manual splitting implements. After preliminary trials, I chose the ten which were the best in their class. With each tool I split a fifth of a cord of wood, where each billet in the fifth was matched for diameter, species, and knottiness by a billet in every other fifth. (Billets matched for knottiness were straight-grained and knot-free, or, if knotty, were selected so that the branch or knot lay in a similar place on each billet.) Therefore, the splitting task was the same for each fifth, permitting comparison between tools. Since I wanted cookstove wood in diameters of three, four, and five inches, this required more work than splitting wood for my wood furnace; there were 180 splits for each fifth. In terms of the measuring device proposed in the first chapter, seven percent of the split sticks fit through the eight-inch hole, fifty percent fit through the six-inch hole, and forty-three percent fit through the four-inch hole. The sixteen-inch billets for my experiment had dried for one year. They ranged in diameter from eighteen inches to four inches. I split every piece over four inches into two, and every piece over eight inches into four. Still larger billets were split more times, often to become the smallest stove sticks.

These rules were governed by a greater rule of splitting: if it splits, split it. The implied reverse is: if it does not split, leave it alone. This general rule is easy to agree with and hard to follow. If a hidden knot running through an entire log makes it extremely difficult to split, I can either keep slamming it to make it come apart anyway, or I can throw it aside. Throw it aside? If this slow compost pile of time-consuming pieces is too painful an idea, I suggest tying up all those crotches and knot-filled pieces with a red ribbon and giving the whole lot to the owner of a fireplace or "chunk furnace" for Christmas. In the experiment, if I had no visible progress on a piece after four blows, I set it aside. There were only three such pieces.

The splitting tools, their list prices, their times for splitting one-fifth of a cord, and their advantages and disadvantages, are discussed below and summarized in Table I. Let's start with the slowest.

Cone-shaped screw mounted on rear wheel of automobile: the Stickler. As the cone turns on the rear hub of my truck, its point screws into the side of a log. The wood, kept from spinning by a bar or other billets on the ground, is wrenched open by the larger diameter of the base of the cone. The two pieces of wood must then be picked off the turning screw and thrown to the side.

When splitting from the top of a billet, the wood cleaves in a path of least resistance. Since the screw enters at the side, the wood has no choice about where it will give, and is bullied into a split. However, the wood shows its displeasure by holding the two split pieces together with several pliable but strong wood fibers. The two pieces must be torn apart by hand to make way for the next piece.[13]

It took over one hour to split my fifth of a cord. Since I required the help of another person to work the gas pedal while I toted wood, this really comes to over two hours of labor, bending over and breathing exhaust the entire time. Toward the end, a billet suddenly shifted off the log supports, spun around with the rotating screw, was thrown to the side, and bruised my arm, a hazard of working closely to the power of my truck.

Wedge sliding on stand (Handy Hammer Splitter II), plus sledge-hammer. A wedge is welded to a steel box, which slides up and down a steel I-beam bolted to a steel stand. You lift the wedge assembly with one hand and set the wood underneath with the other. Then stand back and slam the wedge down with a ten-pound sledgehammer.

If you bang a steel wedge into a billet of wood with a steel hammer, there is a loud ringing sound which is quickly deadened by the wood. However, the vibration in the steel I-beam is not stopped, and after a few minutes of banging, I am sure you too will reach for your hearing protectors.

The Handy Hammer Splitter II is the "heavy duty model," and is a rugged-looking tool. However, after I had split about half a cord (including the fifth from the experiment), the two back seams in the steel box had torn apart by a couple of inches. Another wedge sliding on a stand, the Blue Ox, had been rejected in preliminary trials because it also broke under the strain.

It is hard to miss a wedge which is always in the same place. But for a straight-grained piece of ash or white birch, it's a lot of trouble to lift up the whole wedge assembly (eighteen pounds), jostle the wood into place, let the wedge down on the right spot, then stand back and swing a ten-pound sledgehammer. This extra work is why the fifth of a cord took over fifty-two minutes.

Sledgehammer (eight lb.) and two wedges (four lb. and six lb.). With a wedge in your left hand, and a sledgehammer held near its head in your right hand, whack the wedge into the top of the log three or four times until it is firmly seated. Stand back and swing. You must know where and how deeply to seat your wedge so that you can finish the split with one good stroke. Otherwise, the top-heavy billet will probably tip over and require setting up on the splitting block again. Or you can lay the billet on the ground on its side up against the splitting block and drive the wedge horizontally. The second wedge is for the few times that the first one gets irretrievably stuck down in the billet.

Disadvantages include extra work leaning over, time spent setting a wedge without using the leverage of the sledgehammer handle, and the dangers to hands and feet so close to two colliding hunks of metal (the hazard of flying metal chips is

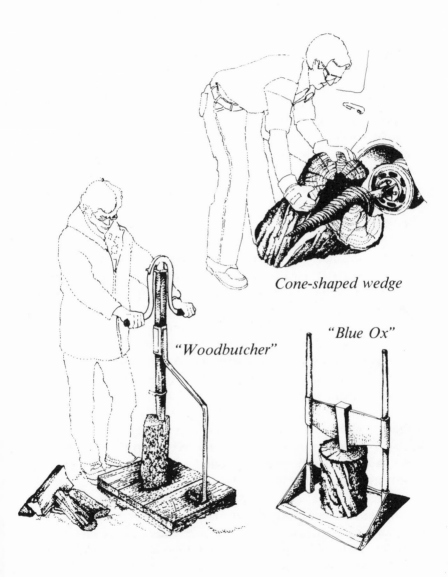

Cone-shaped wedge

"Blue Ox"

"Woodbutcher"

8. *Some modern splitting tools.*

discussed in the section on safety, below). The primary advantage of this splitting method is that you probably own wedges and sledgehammers already for splitting rails or hammering fence posts, and they are the handiest supplements to any of the other tools for splitting wood. By itself, this system took me over forty-nine minutes for a fifth of a cord.

Wedge mounted on stand, no leverage: Woodbutcher. A wedge is welded to a hollow shaft which moves up and down in a frame bolted to a wooden stand. Two handles are attached to a heavy rod inside the wedge shaft; you lift the rod and slam it down on top of the wedge, driving it further with each blow. There is no leverage used except that already given by the length of the arms.

Fetch a billet of wood, lean over with the wood poised in the left hand, lift the wedge assembly with the right hand, with right elbow leaning on right knee for support, tilt the wood into place with the left hand, set the wedge down onto the intended split line. Now straighten up and grasp the two handles with gloved hands. Lift slowly, because too much friction as the rod slides up the shaft will make the wedge lift off the wood; the billet will fall over and must be lifted again. When shoulder height is reached, slam down, *clankngng* . . . And again. And again.

Even with heavy gloves, my hands were bruised; even with hearing protectors, my head rang. I confess I was impressed by how well the Woodbutcher's time for splitting a fifth of a cord compared with other methods (forty-eight minutes, twenty-nine seconds). However, at the end I was soaking with sweat, my lower back was in serious trouble, and I started right in on a fifth of something very different.

Felling ax: 3½ lb. True Temper. Many old-timers have told me that all you need to cleave through wood is a good ax. In olden times, as I indicated previously, axes came in great variety, one common form being a splitting or double-wedge ax to which the old-timers refer. The felling ax is not appreciably fatter behind the edge, and consequently must be occasionally jimmied free when it sticks in the wood.

To turn a tool this light (5¼ lb. total weight) to full advantage requires a slight twist or "twirl" of the handle just as the edge penetrates the wood. This can pop the billet apart, but can also lead to a glancing blow, with ax shooting off to the left and billet to the right. Recent archeological work has shown that many stone axes for splitting had a twist built into their design. The line of the edge was offset from the line of the haft by several degrees, which would convert part of the stroke's energy to a twirl.[14]

My splitting time for a simple ax was forty-six minutes, thirty-one seconds.

Wedge on handle (Blue Waxe), and sledgehammer.   Also taking over forty-six minutes was a thin blue wedge welded to a short steel handle meant to be wielded like an ax or hatchet. This is a lighter tool than all but the ax (6¾ lb. total weight), and shows one just how little force is necessary to split many pieces if the strike is well placed. The Blue Waxe does get stuck, but (unlike the ax) it has been designed to sustain blows from a sledgehammer pushing it through the wood. For larger billets, the Blue Waxe in effect becomes a sledgehammer and wedge method.

Miscellaneous.   Before describing the four best splitters, I should mention six other types of tools that were tested in preliminary trials but rejected for this experiment.

1. The Super Spear comes in many varieties, including the Woodwacker, Quik-Split, and Pogo, all basically a pointed pinch bar or wedge with a sliding ram inside. They work like the Woodbutcher, with the added disadvantage that the tool is not supported by a frame.

2. The Champion Log Splitter is an expensive hand-pumped hydraulic piston worked by four-foot handles. Quartering two logs ten inches in diameter took six minutes, forty-one seconds,

TABLE I. **FIRST TEST OF SPLITTING TOOLS**

SPLITTING TOOL	1980 LIST PRICE	TIME FOR $^1/_5$ CORD (MIN.: SEC.)	WEIGHT WORKED WITH (LBS.)
Hydraulic ram with 10 hp gas engine (Taylor Rental)	$31/day rental fee	30:16 (plus 40 min. pick up and return to rental shop)	————
Standard splitting ax (Snow & Nealley)	$22	34:07	8¾
Heavy triangular headed splitting maul (Sotz Monster Maul)	$23	34:18	15
Ax with hinged separators (Chopper 1)	$33	35:44	7¾
Wedge on handle (Blue Waxe), and sledge-hammer	$19 & $20	46:07	6¾ & 10
Felling Ax ("3½ lb.", True Temper)	$16	46:31	5¼
Wedge mounted on stand, no leverage (Woodbutcher)	$95 & $22 for base	48:29	16, handles; 27, whole wedge assy.
Sledgehammer (8 lb.) and two wedges	$20 & $12	49:36	10, 4, & 6
Wedge sliding on stand (Handy Hammer Splitter II), and sledgehammer	$67 & $20	52:31	18, wedge assy.; & 10
Cone-shaped screw wedge (Stickler) powered by automobile	$175 & auto	60:16 x 2 men (plus 45 min. setup and take down)	————

Advantages	Disadvantages	Estimated Cost for 1 Cord*
protective glasses not necessary; less problem balancing wood; no problems with knots	hearing protectors necessary; no cardio-vascular or stretching exercise	$32.72
not too heavy; maneuverable	protective glasses optional	$24.75
does not get stuck	its weight wears on the operator; protective glasses optional	$24.98
nicely balanced 31¾″ fawn-foot handle	only penetrating ¼″ means some hard knocks; protective glasses optional	$26.52
16″ handle with rubber grip; closer to the work; lighter tool, less effort; good for easy splitting	protective glasses necessary; can be too close to the work when hammer is involved; not effective with knotty pieces	$31.45
you probably need to have this tool around anyway	ax gets stuck and must be jimmied free; protective glasses optional	$29.32
protective glasses not necessary	hearing protectors and gloves necessary; extra pickup at ground level; awkward to set billet in place; lower back much more strained; hands bruised	$40.23
you probably need to have these tools around anyway	protective glasses necessary; too close to the work; flying wedges, metal chips	$32.20
hard to miss a wedge that is always in the same place	protective glasses and hearing protectors necessary; puts you far from the work; strain in setting billet in place; takes more strokes; extra pickup at ground level; weakness in construction	$38.87
protective glasses not necessary	extra pickup at ground level; must tear apart some billets; wood can spin around unexpectedly; working in automobile exhaust	$78.47

* Add splitting and stacking time for one fifth of a cord, multiply by 5, add a portion ($^5/16$) of the pickup or setup time if $3^1/5$ cords will be split at one time, multiply this time by $5/hour labor, then add one tenth the price of the tool or a portion ($^5/16$) of the rental price.

compared to just over a minute with the splitting ax. The Wood-cracker also uses a long lever and ratchet stops to slowly drive a wedge through a billet.

3. A new wedge design called the Wood Grenade features a concave cone shape. The point of this 3¾-lb. cone is supposed to be set in the center of a billet and slammed down with a sledge-hammer, giving the choice of split line to the secrets of the wood. This is fine for the first split, and even increases the incidence of three-way splits (the four-leaf clover of woodsplitting). But what is the center of the next split? I found the Wood Grenade of limited usefulness beyond the first split, and many large billets will not yield at all to the non-directional pressure from the center, often popping the wedge out after every strike of the hammer. As we shall see later, one can learn how to read the face of a billet to know where the weakest cleavage plane is.

4. Another type of wedge (The Quartering Wedge, Ram Rod, Split-Rite, and Quicksplit) has a cross pattern as if two wedges were welded together at right angles. It promises to split each billet into four pieces. Few billets are made without knots or curves; the energy required to force a billet apart along four radii is greater than the energy most people can deliver with a sledgehammer.

5. A new tool which I declined to try (the Woodchuck) has a shaft sliding within a larger pipe. The wedge mounted to the inner shaft slides towards the wedge on the larger pipe through a slot in the larger pipe. The pipe is to be chained to the base of a tree, the shaft bolted to the bumper of a truck; the truck pulls forward, bringing the wedges together and splitting the billet between them. I declined to try this because I felt it to be dangerous to trees and people, and also time-consuming to go forward and back with the truck.

6. Finally, my friend's demonstration of his black gunpowder wedge for tough logs tossed one-half of a billet over the woodshed. I suggested he keep his invention a secret.

THE FOUR BEST

From this experiment, I found that the four fastest tools for woodsplitting—a rented ten-horsepower hydraulic splitter, a Snow & Nealley drop-forged splitting ax, a Sotz Monster Maul, and a Chopper 1 ax—all had times between thirty and thirty-five minutes for splitting a fifth. The next fastest tool, the Blue Waxe, was much slower, taking fifty percent longer than the hydraulic splitter. I chose to concentrate on these four tools, and have repeated the experiment twice, with wood that required 230 splits per fifth.

The splitting times for the matched fifths are given below. Performing the experiment more than once permitted me to see how stable the hierarchy of times remains.

TABLE II. THE FOUR
BEST SPLITTING TOOLS (MIN.: SEC.)

Series	Hydraulic Splitter, 10 HP Gas Engine	Snow & Nealley Splitting Ax	Sotz Monster Maul	Chopper 1 Ax
1. 180 splits/fifth	30:16	34:07	34:18	35:44
2. 230 splits/fifth	40:53	45:29	47:42	51:40
3. 230 splits/fifth	40:44	38:11	42:20	43:34
Average	37:17	39:26	41:44	43:40

Ignoring for the present time taken to travel to the rental store or to maintain each tool, the hydraulic splitter is superior to the Monster Maul and Chopper 1, and the Snow & Nealley maul is superior to the Chopper 1. The other differences are too small for a reliable conclusion.[15] And yet, the Chopper 1 ax takes an average seventeen percent longer than the hydraulic splitter (or three hours, thirty-eight minutes for a cord vs. three hours, six minutes). With an average difference in time between tools being consistent but relatively small, I find myself weighing more heavily how the tool works and how I feel when I use it. I am presenting the observations below for consideration.

Chopper 1. The Chopper 1 ax has the overall shape of a half-wedge ax, with a 31¾-inch fawn-foot helve. It is not made like an ax by heating, drawing, and tempering steel, but rather by casting steel into a special shape with two large holes through the head. Two metal pivoting arms or levers are hinged on one side of the head and protrude on the other side. When the edge of the Chopper 1 penetrates the billet to three-quarters of an inch, these arms engage the split edges of the wood. As it penetrates further, these arms swing to the sides, pushing the wood apart. The design is an exciting new one, although I diasgree that it is "the first new development in wood splitting since the invention of the axe . . . 3 to 4 times better than a conventional axe, splitting maul, or sledgehammer and wedges," as the Chopper 1's advertisements claim. I also find the description of the arms as "spring-loaded" misleading, since the springs do not assist the split, but simply hold the arms to the ax head until they strike the billet. In addition to the ax head, helve, and helve-wedge, there are twelve parts to this device.

When the Chopper 1's splitting mechanism works, the two halves of the billet fly apart ten to twenty feet. It is a terrific sensation. Everyone I have introduced to this tool is thrilled by the explosion. For one thing it means I don't have to pause to toss the two split pieces to the side before setting another billet in place. If I wish to split the billet into smaller pieces, however, I must go that much further to fetch the two halves that have flown off in different directions.

When the billet does not split on the first stroke, the Chopper 1 stops dead at ¾-inch penetration. The shock of this abrupt stop is passed up the handle to my hands. It hurts.

There are a few knotty billets which will open a small distance and no more. In preliminary trials I worked at several such pieces with the Chopper 1 for ten minutes before giving up and

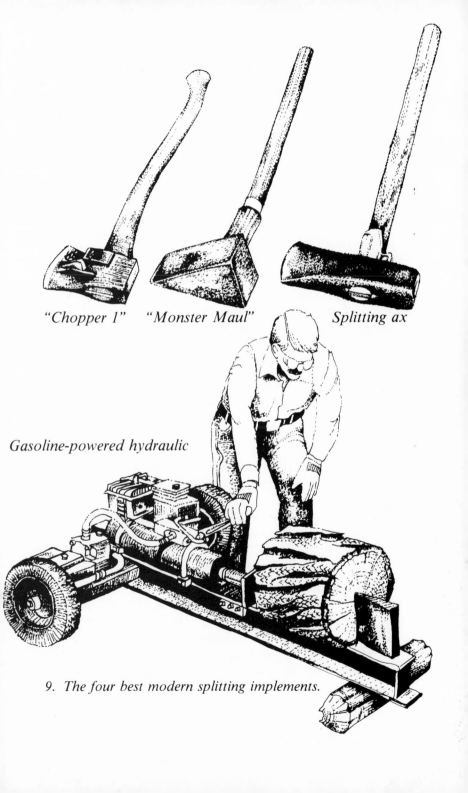

"Chopper 1"   "Monster Maul"   Splitting ax

Gasoline-powered hydraulic

9. *The four best modern splitting implements.*

finishing with the Snow & Nealley splitting ax. A sledgehammer and wedge would also have completed the task.

If there is punk in the end of the billet, the pivot arms have nothing firm to grasp, and will dent rather than split the wood. This is probably why the manufacturer's directions suggest splitting green wood.

Dangers are the same as for a standard splitting ax; that is, if I miss the billet entirely and do not bend my knees, I risk striking myself in the leg. The pivot arms strike the ax head quite hard with each blow, and will , over time, wear down to the breaking point. The moving parts have been known to loosen on occasion. These situations could create a special hazard in using the Chopper 1.

Monster Maul. The Sotz Monster Maul was originally designed as a twenty-three-pound hunk of steel with a blunt edge welded to a 29½-inch handle of steel pipe. The user does not swing it, but rather tries to lift it and let it go. Later, the Sotz Company switched to fifteen-pound mauls of the same design. I have used both, and I quickly abandoned the heavier one in favor of the lighter. Any criticisms of the fifteen-pound maul can be expanded exponentially to apply to the twenty-three-pound maul.

The Monster Maul's head is triangular. The edge is not sharp and will not accidentally cut anyone. The straight sides of the triangle mean the maul never gets stuck in the billet, as will narrower splitting tools. Finally, the maul will stand erect on its large flat head without needing to be balanced against the splitting block.

When splitting a piece of white ash or pine, or any knot-free billet, this much weight is unnecessary, and, after a while, lifting the Monster Maul can be quite tiring. It's my impression that the weight is excessive for knotty pieces, also. Force is the product of mass and acceleration. To increase the splitting force, the Monster Maul design increases the mass. The same force can be attained by swinging a lighter weight more vigorously. When the extra force is not needed, the lighter weight can then be wielded that much more easily, but the Monster Maul's full weight must be hoisted for every split.

A unique safety hazard of the Monster Maul's great weight occurs when the maul drops heavily onto the billet without splitting it. The head then falls on its side. If the head falls off the top of the billet, I am unable to control its course, the weight pulls me after, and my body gets wrenched.

The Monster Maul does not maneuver well in midair, and I have brought it down a few times in the wrong place. The neck of the pipe handle is reinforced, but the pipe has bent along its entire length. I suppose I could take advantage of the manufacturer's ten-year guarantee to send for a new one, but the cost for returning the Monster Maul is several dollars in postage, plus packaging.

Snow & Nealley "Our Best" splitting ax. The standard splitting ax is a rectangular piece of steel drawn to a curved edge. The faces behind the edge are not flat, but have a convex full wedge. The purpose is to drive this fat part down into the wood where it can force the billet apart but not get stuck. The steel is tempered so it will not chip with brittleness or bend with softness. Of all the small differences between the different brands of splitting ax in the shape and quality of the steel, I have found the design and manufacture of the Snow & Nealley the best, and I chose it to represent splitting axes in this experiment.

I find this splitting ax a joy to use. It is light enough (seven-pound head) to maneuver accurately and not to fatigue me, yet it is heavy enough to be accelerated to deliver a great impact if needed. The splitting ax makes a *crack* or *chock* when it splits the wood, compared to the *clunk* of the Monster Maul, and the rattle and bang of the pivot arms opening and hitting the head of the Chopper 1. The danger of missing the billet and swinging the ax all the way around into my foot or leg vanishes if I pay attention to what I am doing, stop splitting when tired, and bend my knees with every stroke. These points of technique are described more carefully in Chapter 4, on poise.

The sharpness of the splitting ax is often neglected, but very important. When dull, the ax is really a maul. When sharpened with file and stone, it cleaves easily.

Hydraulic ram, ten horsepower engine. I have used several of these new gasoline-powered hydraulic woodsplitting machines. I decided my money was best spent renting a powerful $2,000 machine rather than purchasing a weaker and slower "consumer model" for $699. By renting I also do not pay for maintenance or gasoline.

I lay each billet horizontally on a steel I-beam and hold it in place while the piston expands to push the wood to either side of a triangular wedge welded to the opposite end of the I-beam. Then my right hand grasps one half to throw into a pile or set back in place for another split. My left hand holds the hydraulic piston controls in the retract position. I stoop over to pick up a billet, lay it in place, pull the lever, then stoop over to pick up the split wood, then stoop again to pick up another billet. After a while, I find this a strain.

With the manual methods, every stooping to lift weight is followed by stretching in swinging the ax; contraction is followed by lengthening in an unstrained rhythm. I am also invigorated by the cardiovascular exercise I get with the manual methods. I am not invigorated by splitting with the hydraulic splitter. I do not enjoy using it, and must change my attitude while doing so to one of "the end (split stovewood) justifies the means (using the hydraulic splitter)," at least until the job is done.

When I use the hydraulic splitter, I wear hearing protectors to keep out the noise, and feed billets as fast as the splitter will split and retract. I ignore the signs of the wood, which would interest me were I using a splitting ax—the radial cracks in the end of the billet which map out the best approach to a knot, the bulges in the bark to show an old branch site, and so forth.

These signs can be ignored when splitting is powered by a ten-horsepower gasoline engine. I am in danger of becoming so hypnotized or numbed by the noise and the rhythmic in-and-out of the hydraulic piston that my right hand forgets what my left hand is doing. Already very close to the meeting point of wood and wedge, my right hand could get between them. A recent study by three surgeons analyses twenty-three such lacerations and amputations from the 2,200 estimated yearly number of accidents with hydraulic woodsplitters. Less than half of the fingers were successfully replanted. "Nearly all those with residual impairment described cold sensitivity, adding an ironic note to their efforts to conquer the winter."[16]

That a machine can outperform the human body is a common assumption. In each series of splitting trials, however, the gasoline engine was not far ahead of the human-powered tools. In Series 3, I split a fifth of a cord more quickly with the splitting ax than with the hydraulic splitter. Preliminary trials with billets twenty-four inches long indicated that the results would be similar. For longer wood, however, such as four-foot logs for very large furnaces, I expect a hydraulic machine would be superior in the actual splitting time. However, very few mechanical splitters can accommodate billets any longer than two feet long. Besides, larger furnaces require greater girth of wood, and the time and effort to move the wood would increase more quickly than the time saved over splitting by hand.

The hydraulic splitter is very helpful in one situation—when the billets are not cut with a flat face, and so will not stand erect on the splitting block. Much time can be spent setting little wood chips under the short edge of a billet so it will stay still long enough to cleave it in two. In a hydraulic splitter the billet lies on its side, and this nuisance is avoided. Another situation where a hydraulic splitter is helpful is when the wood to split is especially knotty elm, or some gnarled crotches of maple trees. When depending on hand tools, after a few tries, I leave billets in this category to return to the soil. The hydraulic splitter would (probably) cope with them.

SIX MORE CORDS TO BE CERTAIN

I felt I should try the comparison between the splitting ax and the quality hydraulic machine again. I stacked six cords in fifths of a cord, making thirty lots. Each of the thirty was matched with the other twenty-nine in the species, diameter, and knottiness of its billets. This time, I hired two men to do the splitting. One was a wiry fellow of medium build, competent with woodworking tools. The other was an unemployed poet who needed work to pay his rent; he was neither strong nor experienced. I taught them both the skills of the tools to my satisfaction, the second fellow breaking a helve in the learning process. The task was to split and stack a whole cord into stovewood, with 210 splits per fifth. Each man split an entire cord with the splitting ax and an entire cord with the hydraulic machine. To be more realistic about how hydraulic machines are used, I had them split another cord working together. The fair comparison to this seemed to be having both men work on the same cord with splitting axes. The times are shown in Table III.

TABLE III. SPLITTING AND STACKING A CORD OF WOOD USING AX OR MACHINE (MINUTES)

	SPLITTING AX	HYDRAULIC MACHINE
First man	315.94	272.85
Second man	440.22	360.08
Together	185.22	183.00

The first fellow was faster all around; this most efficient of hydraulic splitting machines gave him only a fourteen-

percent reduction in the time taken with the splitting ax. Allowing twenty-five minutes for stacking each fifth, his times were
about the same as mine. The second man was much slower with
the ax, but the hydraulic splitter gave only an eighteen-percent
reduction in the time taken with the ax. Most interesting were
the results from splitting together, which is how I observe
hydraulic splitting machines being commonly used. Compared
with two men working with axes, one of whom is much faster
than the other, there is no appreciable difference between the
performance of the machine and that of the ax.

So how do I conclude the splitting ax is superior? With care,
the ax will last a very long time and can be used a half hour here,
a half hour there, which is indeed much better for the body
than two ten-hour days of hauling and splitting wood.[17] With
the machine, either you own it or rent it. Owning it means a
large investment, and expenditures for gasoline and maintenance of a machine of over three hundred separate parts.
Renting means driving to pick the machine up, an expenditure
of time and gasoline not added to the times in Table III, and
using it to the point of exhaustion in order to complete your
splitting before the rental period is up, then driving it back
again.

A claim from several advertisers of hydraulic splitters which
this series of time-trials dispels is that a cord can be split and
stacked in an hour by one person using a machine. The average
time to stack a fifth of a cord of split wood was twenty-five
minutes. This involved the building of a free-standing pile for
each cord, raised off the ground on shipping pallets, with criss-
cross pillars at both ends leaning slightly toward the center.

I also recorded the times taken to split and stack each of the
fifths in these time-trials; I had expected the splitting and
stacking times to get longer and longer. There was, however,
no pattern I could discern that indicated when the men were
working most or least efficiently.

An informal sort of experiment is a woodsplitting contest

which can be set up at a local fair where different claims can be put to test. The rules of a contest I have run successfully are as follows: Any portable tool, no matter what its source of power, is admitted, although old, damaged equipment may have to be rejected as dangerous. Each pile of billets is about a tenth of a cord, and is matched with those of the other entrants as in the experiments reported above. The billets must be split so that all the sticks fit through a five-inch hole drilled in a piece of plywood. The best time wins; there are four prizes so that more wood will be split, permitting the organizers to raffle off "a cord of split wood" for a local charity. In this way, different tools and techniques can be further compared, and some fun had too.

ECONOMICS

In Table I, I tried to compare the economics of the different splitting techniques. Taking the price of the tool amortized over ten cords, allowing $5/hour for my precious time, assuming I can only operate the rented splitter for an eight-hour day (that's $3^1/_5$ cords without lunch), and adding on twenty minutes to cart and stack each fifth of a cord, I estimated what it might cost to cut and stack a cord of wood. The figures look high, especially compared to the historical costs of a cord of wood "cut, split, and delivered"—$1.20 in 1815, $2.11 in 1880, $3.50 in 1927, and $50 just a few years ago.[18] But I must remember that I need less firewood than, say, the fifty cords that Thomas Jefferson used each winter in the warmer climate of Virginia, that I pay myself more than he did, and that more splitting is required for my cookstove than for my fireplace or furnace. The order of costs to split a cord with these tools is very similar to the order of times, with the dramatic exception of the hydraulic ram. It costs more to split with the rented splitter than with the simpler hand tools.

Our romance of liberation by the machine is very deep. Nearly every farm and garden magazine has featured an article showing how to build one's own gasoline-powered hydraulic splitter, sometimes from scratch. Those people who build these relatively inefficient machines will never catch up with what they could have split by hand while they were building the machines. I know several men and women wood dealers who split by hand several cords of firewood each week to bring in some extra income.

SAFETY

To break wood apart involves powerful vectors of force, particularly at the moment of impact, in unpredicted directions. Most splitting tools carry notices to wear safety goggles in anticipation of flying wood slivers, metal chips from the tools themselves, or stones on the ground. Dead wood is very unpredictable, and, when hit, can send off a spray of small hard wood chips like buckshot. Instead of cheap plastic goggles, I prefer safety spectacles made of polycarbonate safety glass for workers in industry who must wear them all day. I find these to be much more comfortable than plastic goggles, which fog up when I begin to exert effort, and which scratch easily, further clouding my vision.

Striking the foot with the splitting ax is another safety problem. The circles of swing, illustrated in the Poise chapter, can bring the ax not far from the feet. The best prevention against accidents, and the most effective and comfortable method of splitting, employs a large sturdy splitting block, which sets the top of the billet at the height of the waist, the height of the block being about twenty inches. Some woodsmen suggest turning a log onto its side, leaning the billet against it, and holding the billet in place with the foot. Then they warn that extreme caution is necessary. The brain is not capable of the "extreme caution" necessary to react in the milliseconds between a twisted or glancing blow and impact of ax into foot. With the block, the energy is spent in the wood and block, knees are bent, and the ax drops straight down a safe distance from the feet.

Another very good reason for using a splitting block is that the body can remain erect. The hardest part of splitting wood is moving it, and this is the part of the task where most care must be taken. While hoisting the wood to a splitting block entails more work, it puts the billet in a position less demanding on the body. When the ax contacts the billet, the force is directed downward with gravity. Leaning over to split wood on the ground, however, results in forward and backward forces on the body, which in an extended posture are very hard on the small of the back. The key to lifting the wood, or any heavy weight, is to keep the weight as close as possible to the vertical axis of the body, while bending at the knees and hip joints to use the more powerful muscles of the legs (see Moving Wood in Chapter 4).

Gloves for the hand give an added cushion for unexpected shocks, are useful for protecting against splinters when picking up wood, and give warmth in winter. They should not be very thick, since strength and sensitivity of grip are lost with thick gloves.[19]

After splitting for a while, I occasionally overshoot my mark at the edge of the billet. Occasionally the wood splits unevenly in this situation and the part of the helve nearest the ax head strikes the wood. If I set the ax head completely off the far end of the billet, this impact can break the helve in two. More often, such a strike will injure the helve and loosen the head. A loose or detached head is dangerous, and replacing a broken helve is a nuisance; these should be avoided. Greater care in placing the strike is the best prevention. Some sort of wrapping to protect the portion of the helve directly below the ax head is another preventive measure. Such wrappings can be made from an old tire, inner tube, or from a piece of sheet metal tacked to the helve. A rubber sleeve is sold for this purpose, but I have found that this design does not fit all helves and that it crumbles apart after repeated accidents. An adjustable handle guard of sheet steel has a screw to tighten its grip to the helve; when struck it can dent but will not need replacement (shown in Figure 9).

The ax head occasionally loosens on the helve, sometimes

10. Studying the mechanics of woodsplitting.

unexpectedly, from the effects of seasonal changes in relative humidity. Other people should not be in front or behind when you are splitting. Children who help by picking up and stacking wood have been the victims of various types of flying objects. To keep them participating but out of the way until the splitter takes a rest, let them study the mechanics of woodsplitting with the toy in Figure 10.

To tighten the ax head, hold the ax with head up and tap the butt of the helve down on the splitting block. The momentum of the head seats it securely on the helve. Then hammer the helve-wedge in more tightly or add another wedge. Some woodsmen suggest soaking the head in water so the wood will swell and tighten the fitting, but this will assure a loose handle unless the handle and head are kept wet at all times, and will eventually rot the handle. To prevent a helve from shrinking, excess moisture should be wiped off after each use, and the helve near the eye wiped with a light oil. A plastic bag can be put over the head, and the ax stored off the ground in a dry shed.

When you are carrying an ax to the place of work, the ax should be held close to the head perhaps with an edge cover (Figure 13). The safe way to carry an uncovered ax is the solution to an old riddle of Eastern Europe: "I go from home, it looks home; I come from the meadow, it looks at the meadow."[20] Earlier in America a sling was used to cover the edge and hang the ax over the shoulder for carrying long distances (Figure 11).

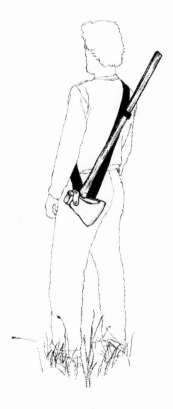

11. The ax sling.

Sometimes the splitting ax gets stuck in the top of the billet. Then I lean over to push down with my left hand while prying loose with my right hand. Occasionally the ax suddenly pops out toward my face, rising a foot or more from the wood. Broken teeth have been reported from this type of encounter. A preventive measure is to keep the left arm straight so the face is not close to the wood. Another preventive measure is to know reaction wood, the type of wood that has this extra spring to propel ax heads upward. Reaction wood is the tree's response to injuries and to the weight of branches, as well as to the effects of gravity on a leaning portion of the tree. In hardwoods, reaction wood most often occurs as tension wood on the upper side of a leaning tree or opposite a heavy branch, in conifers, as compression wood on the underside.

WEDGES

With safety glasses, splitting block, light-weight gloves, and handle guard, I thought I had solved the major safety problems of splitting wood. To make sure, I contacted the supervising nurses in the emergency rooms of five New England hospitals. Short of actually going through the doctors' and hospitals' records, consulting these inividuals, who know more than anyone about the kinds of serious accidents that occur in their areas, seemed the best way to learn of the real hazards of woodsplitting. Of course, their worst stories were about chain-saws. For splitting wood, the most frequent accident reported was a metal chip from an ax or wedge flying off at great speed and imbedding itself in the fleshy parts of the body, something like shrapnel. So the safety glasses were not enough! Should I wear armored pants and shirt? This problem requires a better solution.

When metal strikes metal, some of the energy of the strike

goes into remolding the metal. After a shorter or longer time, a higher-quality wedge will mushroom out to the sides, eventually breaking into pieces. Some of these will fall harmlessly, and some will fly off with a great part of the strike's energy. Splitting ax heads, too, can chip, though they are made of a harder steel than wedges, since their task is primarily cutting wood. Striking the poll of a light felling ax can bend and break the eye. But it is hard steel or cast steel wedges that are especially brittle and prone to sending off chips. Brittleness in axes and wedges is much worse on a very cold day. Loggers traditionally warmed their axes before work, and the same can be done with splitting tools normally stored outside.

The protruding edges of the mushroom on a well-used wedge are obviously prone to coming all the way off, and must be filed or ground down. However, only the ends of steel wedges are tempered for the optimum hardness characteristics, and once this area is filed away, the wedge deteriorates more rapidly. Indeed, the process of grinding produces enough heat to ruin the remaining temper of the wedge's metal. I have seen wedges used many years with very little deformation, a happy coincidence of the right consistency of steel, the right temper, and careful use, but these are the exceptions.

Proper repair or "redressing" of a deformed tool involves:

1. Testing for internal fatigue failure. In the magnaflux method, the metal is magnetized and covered with a fine magnetic powder; in the vicinity of an internal crack there is a disturbance of the magnetic flux, and the powder gathers there. Flawed tools must be rejected.

2. Grinding with a fine grit wheel kept wet by a dripping tin of water at a low speed to ensure low temperature.

3. Relieving stress by heating at five hundred degrees for an hour, and perhaps reannealing at higher temperatures.

These redressing procedures seem absurd for the average splitter of firewood. Seeking an alternative, I discovered there

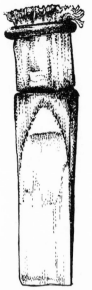

wood-and-steel socket   *wood glut*   *steel*

serrated steel   *conical*   *steel, chipped and mushroomed*

12. Wedges.

were four traditional methods used in Europe for splitting wood, in every case avoiding the impact of metal upon metal.

1. The first is to split with a splitting ax. If the ax gets stuck part way through a split, it is pounded with a wooden mallet called a beetle (or cudgel or sometimes maul, shown in Figures 13 and 14), made from a burl or root-crown of a tree.

2. A wedge is pounded with a beetle. The groove in steel wedges is to prevent the wedge popping out of frozen or reaction wood, and occasionally sand is used to increase the friction between edge and wood. One type of steel wedge, called Schnucke's toothed wedge, has serrations pointing upwards, and was used in Europe in the nineteenth century (Figure 12).

3. A wooden wedge of beech or hornbeam (sometimes called a glut) is driven into a small cleft begun with the ax. This has worked well for moderately tenacious billets. But as Publius Syrus said in the first century BC, "Look for a tough wedge for a tough billet," and my preference for most situations requiring a wedge goes to the final type of wedge.

4. The most used type of wedge for driving with the ax has been a socket wedge, a sharp steel edge ending in a hollow socket into which fits a wooden insert (Figure 12). The sledgehammer or poll of the splitting ax strikes the wooden insert, avoiding the problems of metal striking metal. The wooden insert is prevented from splitting apart by a steel ring; the wood mushrooms out against the ring more and more tightly, eventually wearing down. At that point the wedge is not discarded as is the all-steel wedge; rather, a new wooden insert is fitted to the socket. Concerned that the wooden insert would wear out quickly, I recalled that circus tents in my boyhood were held up by durable wooden stakes collared with a small steel ring: a traveling circus seems an excellent judge of efficiency in materials. So too the large chisels of post-and-beam construction, with wooden handles secured with a steel hoop.[21]

The ring on a new wood-and-steel wedge should be seated about an inch from the top and the wood pounded down a bit around its edges to hold the ring in place. With the amount of force put out by the poll of the splitting ax, the wood will soon mushroom over quite nicely. Any wedge can get stuck in an old gnarly crotch. That is more serious with the wood-and-steel wedge since it is more fragile from the side; freeing it by hitting it on the side may dislodge the wooden insert. The wood can be inserted again if it has not been banged to pieces. Rescuing the stuck wedge with another wedge set further along in the crack is a better technique.

In my tests of the wood-and-steel socket wedge, I have been pleased with the longevity of the parts, and pleased with the extra margin of safety they afford. A drawback is that not as much of the ax head's energy is delivered to the operation of splitting: the same resilience of wood which I find so important in a helve dissipates some of the energy of the ax head striking the wood-topped wedge. It is a small price to pay for the increased safety.

SHARPENING

Iron is the father of fire and stone its mother.
—Old saying from Siberia[22]

Most splitting can be done with the splitting ax unassisted by other tools. But, if not sharp, it beats the wood, is less safe, and should be called a "maul." Traditionally, axes were sharpened with files, whetstones, or both. For filing, the ax should be clamped in a vise, and the mill bastard file pushed from three inches back from the edge off the end of the ax. The file should be lifted for the return stroke. Circular grindstones turned by foot treadle were common not too long ago. A tin of water dripped onto the ax as the wheel slowly turned to avoid the heat that would ruin the temper. When the grindstone broke in the lumber camp of Paul Bunyan, America's king logger, the axmen carried boulders to the top of the mountain, let them loose, and ran behind, holding their axes to the top of the rolling stones. Smaller round ax stones can be easily carried in the pocket to be used when needed.

An ax does not need a razor-sharp edge. Far more important is to retain the optimum shape of the wedge, a convex bevel beginning a few inches from the edge and running smoothly to the edge, as in Figure 5, a shape which can be felt with thumb and forefinger.

The lumberman's advice to "grind your ax until the blade is so sharp and thin the sun can shine through it"[23] is to be taken literally only as far as the smooth reflectiveness of the surface; it is more a symbolic statement about the sun's energy in the ax, put to best use when it is sharp.

PREPARING FIREWOOD FOR SPLITTING: FELLING AND BUCKING

Commonly selecting one of the most noble, for the first trial of his power, he would approach it with a listless air, whistling a low tune; and wielding his ax, with a certain flourish, not unlike the salutes of a fencing master, he would strike a light blow into the bark, and measure his distance. The pause that followed was ominous of the fall of the forest, which had flourished there for centuries. The heavy and brisk blows that he struck were soon succeeded by the thundering report of the tree, as it came, first cracking and threatening . . . finally meeting the ground with a shock but little inferior to an earthquake.

—James Fenimore Cooper
The Pioneers, 1823

Splitting firewood depends on the exposure of the tree's endgrain by felling and bucking. In general, an undercut is first made at the base of the tree on the side toward which the tree is to fall. Then the felling cut is made on the opposite side, a little above the undercut and coming down toward it. Before the tree is cut through entirely, it falls, the last intact fibers acting as a hinge, keeping the butt from slipping off the stump. Once down, the tree is cut into sections, or bucked, the lengths depending on the intended use of the wood and means whereby it is to be taken from the woods.

Woodsmen sometimes took two or three types of axes into the forests for the different tasks of felling, trimming branches, and cutting to length. The care of the tool and the technique of its use are similar to those of the splitting ax described in this book. The dangers of bringing a large tree from vertical to horizontal are lessened by the slowness and quiet of the ax, in comparison to the racket of the chainsaw, since movement of the tree's mass can be seen and heard by the axman in time for a hasty retreat.

Axes were displaced by saws, especially when bucking. A saw is a series of knives, each knife taking a tiny piece of wood away or scoring the wood so a blunt raker tooth can scrape a small piece away. Bucking saws have been used for at least six thousand years. Felling saws, usually four to six feet long, but as much as sixteen feet long for the huge trees of the West, have been in use for about two hundred years. One-person and two-person crosscut saws have today been displaced by gasoline-powered chainsaws, though it has only been within the last few years that a competent chain-saw operator could outcut a competent crosscut sawyer.

Care and use of crosscut saws and chainsaws is much more complicated than the how-to-fell-trees books and advertisements claim. The chainsaw has over three hundred parts, is heavy, noisy, extremely dangerous, and also very useful in skilled and cautious hands. The crosscut saw is at the center of a tool system and tradition involving several other tools, particularly those to set and sharpen with

accuracy the saw's cutting and cleaning teeth. Several books
introduce these tools well, but give a wrong sense of
confidence to a new woodsman. Even experienced professionals
are occasionally taken to the hospital, victims of "kickback,"
"deadfalls," or "widowmakers." Perhaps most important to
tree-felling is a knowledge of what to cut and how to bring it
down without damaging its vegetable or human neighbors, a
knowledge best gained in the woods with guidance. It is said in
England, "More harm can be done in half an hour by an un-
skilled woodcutter than can be put right in years."[24]

The arts of splitting and crosscutting differ in technique
as well as in tools. Splitting means finding natural cleavage
planes, or the bodily joints of the wood. Crosscutting means
working against the structure of the wood, placement of the
cut being determined by convenience to the woodsman.
Thus crosscutting is a matter of human planning and
human whim, sometimes leading to the sort of arrogance
described in the quote at the beginning of this section. In
splitting, a close reading of the structure of the wood
increases efficiency, whereas arrogance reduces efficiency.
In splitting, one well-placed strike completes the work.
Crosscutting requires repeated strikes of the ax or saw, and
can be accompanied by work chants that coordinate the
rhythm, especially when two or more people are working
together. With splitting, the work pace is set by the rhythm
of the heart, and one must sing to oneself. In cultures which
use only axes, as I have mentioned above, the actions of
cutting and splitting overlap, and trees are harvested
completely at one time with many similar movements. Thus
these distinctions are strongest when saws are used for
cutting, and are blurred when only axes are used to cut and
split.

Crosscutting can release an unseen tension in a tree,
initiating an unexpected split for all or part of its length for
which the cutter is not prepared. While this is most common

when felling, the following quote describes such an accident, fictional but based on the author's experience, that happened when lumbermen were bucking a fir tree with a chainsaw in the Pacific Northwest. It is the best expression I know of the rapidity with which huge masses of wood can move, making the idea of human preparedness worthless.

> . . . listen! the maddened snapping of bark someplace else moving, he turns back to the log in time to see a bright yellow-white row of teeth appear splintering over the mossy lips to gnash the saw from his hands fling it furiously to the ground it claws screaming machine frenzy and terror trying to dig escape from the vengeful wood just above where Old Henry drops his screwjack *Gaw* when mud and pine needles spray over him like black *damn!* rain an' even if I don't see so clear as I used to there's still time to get down the hill Joe Ben hears the metal scream behind a curtain of fern but if you never doubt in your mind where's Hank spins away leaving his log and turn . . . to see the log springing suddenly massive upright pivots on Henry's arm God my good one goddammit . . . it waves limp then disappears a second beneath the row of teeth before the log springs on downhill massive upright like the bastard is trying to stand up again and find its stump! a swinging green fist slams Hank's shoulder goes somersaulting past upright like the bastard is so mad getting chopped down it jumps up chews off the old man's arm clubs me one tearing off downhill . . .[25]

KINDLING

To kindle means to give birth, and is related to *kin* and *kinder* (German for children). Thus kindling is the wood used to give birth to the fire. Anciently, a "male" stick was twirled in a depression in a "female" stick of another species to start a fire; likewise small sticks added to the first flames were thought of as "male" (giving off flames) or "female" (receiving and spreading flames), depending on their size and species. The critical girth of a stick above which it cannot sustain this birth of fire without the aid of supplementary heat is ¾-inch diameter, and the combustion must be fed with pieces only a little larger.[26] Other food to help a fire grow can consist of dry leaves, corncobs, straw, and/or paper. (Colored paper should be avoided since it has enough heavy metals to make the ashes a hazardous waste rather than a helpful addition to the garden.)

Making sticks or small billets into kindling is so special a form of splitting that it has its own tools and techniques. To compare these tools, I had to first decide what the ideal girth of kindling was. I made another board with holes in it (like the one in Figure 3), with holes 3, 2⅝, 2, and 1⅝ inches in diameter. My subjective sense of what kindling ought to be was satisfied only by sticks which were small enough to fit through the two-inch hole, seen around the block in Figure 14. Of course, kindling can be as small as shavings for the very beginning of the fire, and the youngsters of the household once upon a time spent some of their day collecting chips from around the splitting block. But for the purpose of this comparison, at least two inches small was adequate.

The four tools I compared for making kindling were the splitting ax, a medium-length felling ax (helve twenty-six inches from the head), a hatchet with a knob at the end of the helve to prevent slipping out of the hand, and a froe with club. The froe (or frow, Figures 13 and 14) is inherited from the Romans, and is the traditional tool for riving clapboards, shingles, fence rails, barrel staves, and ax helves. Not tested were the various styles of English billhook (or the American version, the "Woodman's Pal").

To split with any of the three axes, the stick is held with

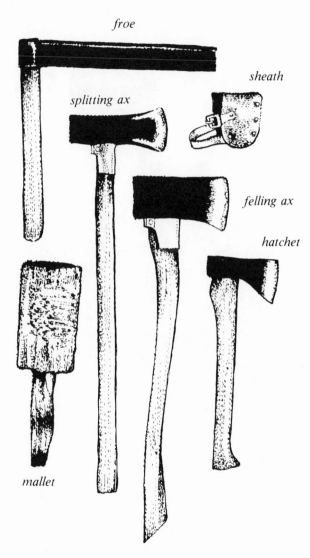

13. Tools for kindling.

14. Froe and mallet in use.

one hand. To avoid hurting fingers, the left hand, heavily
gloved, lets go the instant before the ax strikes. Such
coordination is easier described than achieved, most injuries
coming from overconfidence and a lapse of razor-sharp
attentiveness.[27] Rudolph Hommel observed in China elderly
women squatting with cleavers fashioned with a spike
extending downward from the tip. The sticks were held

from the base, the spike hit the ground at the end of the strike, the blade never hit the ground or the fingers.[28]

With the two smaller axes, the stick can be tapped just hard enough to set the ax head in the stick. The best way to do this is for one hand to hold the stick against the edge of the ax, which is held by the other hand. Ax and stick, in contact, are lifted a few inches above the block and brought down hard to set the edge where you want it. With the ax set in the stick, both hands can lift the ax and bring it down on the splitting block with enough force to complete the split. Or ax-set-in-stick can be turned upside-down and the poll brought down on the block; the momentum of the stick splits it. Such techniques are foolhardy when splitting large billets.

For this task, the splitting ax feels cumbersome—it becomes the Monster Maul of kindling. Yet it gets the job done, and a good case can be made for making kindling while splitting firewood when one has found a billet that splits easily (one that has great "fissibility," a term I like).

Instead of a three- or four-inch edge, the froe has fifteen inches. The handle rises at a right angle behind the edge and is held to guide the blade while the other hand holds a club to knock the part of the blade extending beyond the wood, thus driving the whole thing forward. For riving clapboards, the froe is worked back and forth at right angles to the plane of the split in order to wrench the wood apart. But for short pieces of firewood, the blade is driven straight along the grain. The most important feature of this design is that the hand not holding the tool is *behind* the cutting edge, out of harm's way. Judging from the nicked and severed fingers experienced by amateurs and old-timers alike, this seems to be an important precaution.

The froe can also be wielded like a small ax, swinging it onto the top of a stick. Or, embedding the edge in the stick, both can be raised and then slammed down upon the block.

A froe is a simpler tool than an ax, often just a steel bar with a sharpened edge. This edge seems to be always dull when new, and needs to be filed and ground for best efficiency.

The times required to split similar volumes of hardwood kindling are given in Table IV.

TABLE IV. SPLITTING KINDLING WITH FOUR TOOLS

Tool	Time (min.)	Volume split (cubic feet)	Volume unsplit (cubic feet)	Minutes per cubic foot
Splitting ax	134.80	11.96	.89	11.27
Medium felling ax	114.98	10.07	2.39	11.42
Hatchet	114.08	10.00	2.68	11.41
Froe (and club)	156.33	11.64	1.33	13.43

The sixteen-inch sticks were carefully matched at the beginning of the trials, but came out at the end with somewhat different volumes, probably because of variations in stacking. The minutes required with each tool to produce a cubic foot of kindling are remarkably similar, the froe requiring somewhat more time. The volume of wood that could not be split further because of limitations of the tool was greater for the two quarter-wedge axes. It seems that the decision about what tool to use in splitting kindling depends on personal preference, considerations of safety, and versatility.

3. Where and When to Split: Six Common Myths about Splitting Firewood

The art of splitting requires more attention to the structure of the wood than does crosscutting. We speak of scientists splitting atoms, not cutting them, to show our regard (and hope) for the scientists' ability to find the ways in which the atoms come apart most easily. Similarly a Taoist Chinese cook, whose blade has lasted a hundred times longer than his lesser colleagues', speaks not of cutting meat but of sensing the natural divisions of the flesh. "I press the big tendons apart and follow along the big openings, conforming to the lines which must be followed."[1]

For the task of splitting firewood several hints promise how to save time and effort. These hints concern when to split, how freshly cut the wood should be for best splitting, what species to prefer, how to approach the billet or log, and so forth. I call these hints common myths because they are passed down from woodsman to woodsman without verification, lasting on the strength of tradition. I cannot rely on subjective impressions to prove or disprove the hypothesis of a common myth. For one thing, I always seem to recall the exceptionally easy or hard pieces from my woodsplitting past, and so I do not get a very accurate general picture. Simple experiments are useful for sorting out different factors objectively. With this in mind I set out to test whether or not the following six common myths about woodsplitting were true.

MYTH NUMBER 1: SPLIT FROM THE BOTTOM, NOT FROM THE TOP

According to one authority, the basic rule of woodsplitting is to split up the grain. In other words, put the end growing toward the sky down onto the splitting block with branches pointing earthward. As the authority stated, "The tree grew this way, the grain flows this way. Splitting down the grain is the commonest error a beginner will make, and will make even the easiest wood difficult to split."[2] I was quite surprised to read this, since the old-timers I use as consultants had said, "Always split from the top down, just the way the tree grows." I wondered if I had followed the wrong advice, and if turning those well-remembered hard pieces upside down would have made it all easier.

To test which way would be best, I got together thirty-six pairs of billets, all sixteen inches long, to be split for stovewood. Each pair was matched for species, diameter, knottiness, and number of splits. The splitting of each billet was timed. The average time difference was just over one hundredth of a second per split in favor of the bottom facing up. For a cord of cookstove wood requiring upwards of a thousand splits, this might mean a difference of ten seconds or so overall. Since the average time to split just one billet into stovewood was forty-eight seconds, such a minuscule effect would surely be swamped by just one piece which took longer than expected. The common myth is wrong; it does not matter which end you approach.

MYTH NUMBER 2: SPLIT ALONG THE CHECK LINES

After seasoning for a few weeks, a billet will begin to show cracks called check lines, emanating outward from the center of the cut end (see Frontispiece). These checks or cracks occur because the wood when drying shrinks twice as much in the tangential plane (the plane parallel to the pith but not passing through it) as in the radial plane (emanating outward from the center). The ruptures appear in the bundles of horizontal ray parenchyma cells radiating from the center. Ray parenchyma cells are routes of horizontal transport of nutrients and account for from five to thirty percent of the tree's volume, more in branchwood than in the trunk.[3] "Frost cracks" (caused by disease, not by frost) are another sort of check and usually run right through to the center of the billet.[4]

A common assumption is that checks indicate the planes of greatest weakness and should guide the splitting ax. However, we know that the appearance of the end of a log is not a reliable indicator of its internal moisture;[5] might checks as hints about internal structure also be misleading?

For forty-seven hardwood billets seasoned six months and forty-eight billets cut two weeks previously, I marked all the drying checks longer than one-third the radius of the end. I drilled a quarter-inch hole in the very center of the billet and hammered in a radially symmetrical wedge that exerted pressure equally in every direction. Ninety billets split along the largest crack; the other five split along the second largest crack. This common myth is confirmed.

I cannot answer the question *how much* less resistance there is in these planes indicated by the check lines. But I can say that they provide an excellent map for dealing with knots. Sometimes the check lines direct me to drive straight through the center of a branch, and sometimes to the side. Even in crotches, where the reaction wood around a junction of two branches is partially gnarled, the cracks are right. When I ignore the advice of the cracks and compare with those times the advice was taken, I realize that a moment spent reading the signs of the wood is well repaid in efficiency and enjoyment.

Very large billets are an exception to the rule that cracks guide the splitter. Often the best approach is to split away a series of

15. Splitting large billets by secant sectioning.

secant sections from the perimeter, the split line being tangential to the growth rings. Called "daisy-making," this produces a billet that looks like a radish cut to garnish a salad (Figure 15).

MYTH NUMBER 3: FROZEN GREEN WOOD SPLITS EASIEST

I had always been told that frozen wood splits easier because water turned to ice inside the billet makes the billet stiffer and more brittle, thus more likely to crack than to bend. Thus green wood, with a higher moisture content, would be especially easy to split when frozen.

A minority opinion was that frozen wood was stronger—wood in fact gains 2-5 percent in strength for every ten degree drop in temperature. One old-timer told me that as a youth he had played a wedge-popping game in the winter. A stump was split part way and a wooden wedge driven in the cleft. When the side of the stump was struck with the poll of the ax, the wedge would pop up sometimes twenty feet into the air. The old-timer reasoned that this greater tenacity in frozen wood made it harder to split.

To test this common myth, I set up twenty-five groups of four billets each, totalling 100 billets. Within each group, the four billets were sixteen inches long and matched for diameter, species, and knottiness. One of the four was freshly cut and was set out to freeze hard; one was green and thawed indoors; one had dried under cover for seven months and was frozen; one was dry and thawed. I split all these pieces in a random sequence, with a friend recording the time it took to split each billet into stovewood.

I was amazed to find out that frozen wood split no more quickly than thawed wood, that green wood split no more quickly than seasoned wood, and that straight-grained knot-free pieces split only a little more quickly than knotty pieces (8.52 vs. 9.82 seconds per split).

It appeared that knotty pieces split somewhat more quickly when thawed and straight-grain pieces more quickly when frozen. There is an average difference of more than three seconds per split between knotty thawed wood (8.17 seconds per split) and knotty frozen (11.48 seconds). This can add up to fifty minutes difference in a cord—if knotty pieces are all that I am splitting.

The difference is less for straight-grained pieces; an average of 8.08 seconds per split when the knot-free pieces are frozen vs. 8.97 seconds when they are thawed. Assuming a thousand splits per cord for the smaller-caliber firewood needed by a cookstove, this comes to two hours and fourteen minutes for frozen knot-free wood, rather than two hours and twenty-nine minutes for thawed knot-free wood.[6]

The myth that frozen wood splits easiest is partly confirmed and partly disconfirmed. Considering the mixture in my wood-pile of knotty and knot-free pieces of different species and diameters, it makes more sense to split firewood when I have the time and energy than it does to wait for certain temperatures to split certain types of wood. The time taken to sort the billets into separate piles would more than offset any advantages achieved by waiting.

MYTH NUMBER 4: SEASON FIREWOOD ONE YEAR, BETTER TWO YEARS

Excessive smoke, creosote, and inefficient burning are three important reasons for not burning green wood, but too-dry wood can be a problem as well, since too-rapid combustion can also lead to incomplete burning and creosote formation. Proper moisture level of fuelwood is far more important for burning efficiency than firebrick liners, secondary air inlets, and baffles in the stove. Jay Shelton, a researcher on wood fuel efficiencies, suggests the optimum range is 15–30 percent moisture, where 100 percent means half water and half wood by weight (the usual condition of green wood).[7]

I have heard many estimates of the time it takes wood to dry; the most conservative (one to two years) is the most often expressed. To test this idea, Tom Gajda, in a research project at the University of Massachusetts in Amherst, measured the moisture contents of logs in different lengths (four-, two-, and one-foot), split once or unsplit, and in three species (red oak, white birch, and red maple). This added up to eighteen categories with about ten logs apiece. Gajda weighed the 185 logs at 36-day intervals commencing March 18 and ending November 1.[8]

According to Gajda's results, I can fell a tree in early March when internal moisture is still low, and have the wood ready for the stove in November—if at the time that the tree is felled I cut it to two- or one-foot lengths, or split it, or both, and stack it off the

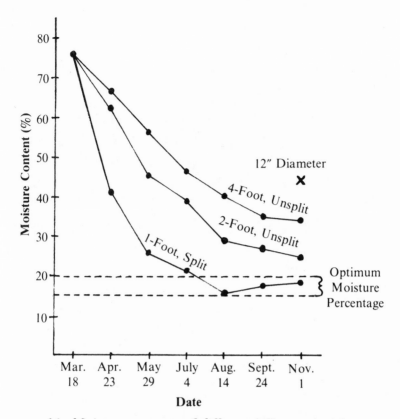

16. Moisture contents of different billets and sticks.

ground in a covered woodpile. If I wait to cut the wood to length or to split it, I may not be able to achieve the optimum moisture content before the burning season. Figure 16 shows how moisture is lost in three different preparations of firewood. Lines for two-foot split and for one-foot unsplit billets would be sandwiched between the bottom two lines.

Myth Number 4 holds true if the wood is kept in long pieces of large diameter. Myth Number 4 is wrong if the firewood is cut to stove length, or split, or both, and stored up off the ground in a covered woodpile. A reason to hurry is that a higher moisture content invites the fungi and bacteria, who use the wood's energy for their own livelihood (Figure 17), leaving less for warming humans. Since fungi become particularly active when moisture in

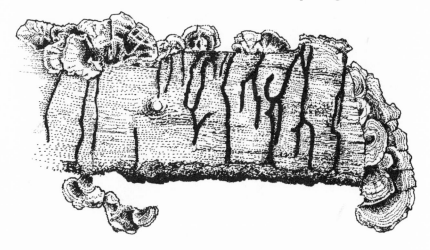

17. Competitors for the wood's energy.

wood is greater than twenty percent, the optimum range for seasoned wood is narrowed from 15–30 percent in Shelton's tests to 15–20 percent.

The graph in Figure 16 can be used as a general drying guide for firewood. Adjustments must be made for date of felling, geographical location, and diameter of tree. If the wood is cut later in the spring or summer, there may be more water in the tree and the best drying months of April and May would have been missed; add ten percentage points for each month of delay. The reverse is not true: trees cut in the dead of winter are frozen and lose moisture very slowly. In areas with higher average temperatures, wood will dry more quickly.

Wood comes to a point of equilibrium where it no longer loses moisture because the surrounding air is moist. The "equilibrium moisture content" cannot go below twenty percent (our limit for seasoned wood) when the relative humidity is eighty-five percent or over. Two related common myths—"April rains on the woodpile pull the moisture out," and "One year of drying for every inch of thickness"—are observations of seasonal changes in relative humidity. In areas where the relative humidity is different from New England's 70–80 percent, these two common myths are no longer true. In drier climates, drying proceeds more rapidly. In Judea, wood cut the previous winter was ready by the Fifteenth Day of Ab in August, when a year's supply of split wood was brought to the altar in the Festival of Woodbearing.

Another variable in the rate of drying is the technique of stacking. Gajda's sticks were a full twelve inches off the ground to avoid the wetness of the earth and increase air circulation up through the pile. I use shipping pallets set on scrap boards under

18. *A well-built woodpile.*

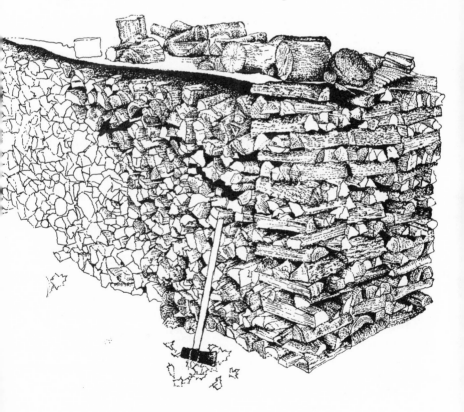

all my firewood; while they do not elevate the wood twelve inches, a disadvantage for which I must allow more drying time, the pallets allow some circulation from the bottom. Some people stack all their sticks in criss-cross fashion, creating a group of chimneys to maximize air movement. I make these criss-cross stacks at the ends of my free-standing stacks to hold the piles together, but I feel it is too consuming of space and time to stack all my wood that way. The spaces between sticks lying together are more than adequate for ventilation. One secret of stacking is that at every level of the criss-cross pillar, the sticks must be placed tightly together so that they will not roll and topple the wood above them. Another secret is that the stack must lean toward the center from every direction. If two or more rows are stacked together, they should be spaced apart several inches at the base, a gap which is closed by the top of the pile. A woodshed reduces the time spent in restacking free-standing woodpiles that have settled and fallen over, but should also have a means of air circulation from the bottom.

Gajda's sticks were covered on the top with sheet metal to avert rain without hindering the passage of air. Some people cover their wood in plastic. When it drapes over the sides, moisture cannot escape and the pile becomes a fungi culture chamber. When the sun shines, the plastic becomes brittle; when the wind blows, it tears, letting the rain in. I prefer scraps of boards or metal to keep rain out.

Spring is a poor time to cut wood because the relative humidity is higher. The moisture content of the wood is also higher as the sap begins to run. The extreme case is yellow birch, which has a ninety percent moisture content in late April compared to fifty percent in September. In traditional China, woodchopping was prohibited in April and part of May presumably for this reason. Most hardwoods, however, change only a few percentage points in moisture content from one time of year to another, averaging 81.4 percent for heartwood and 82.7 percent for sapwood (softwoods average 55.4 percent moisture in heartwood and 148.9 percent in sapwood).[9]

The diameter of Tom Gajda's logs was six-and-a-half inches. When split once, they would qualify for fireplace and furnace wood (from Figure 2). Billets of larger diameter will dry just as quickly if split to the same girth, and more quickly if split to a smaller girth, but will dry more slowly if not split. Adjustment factors based on the different ratios of surface area to volume give good estimates. In Figure 16 I have included one such point for a piece twelve inches in diameter, unsplit, and four feet long.[10]

To summarize, it is best to fell trees between late autumn and early spring, to limb and buck them at that time, to split them in a week or two when check lines appear, then to stack and cover until the following fall or winter.

For greater accuracy in producing the highest quality firewood, the actual moisture content of firewood can be measured easily. Since wet or green wood is only sixty percent as efficient a fuel as optimally seasoned wood, it seems that moisture should be tested more often. To determine the moisture content of a piece of wood, a wafer weighing one or two pounds should be cut from the center of the piece and quickly sealed in a locking plastic bag. This wafer is weighed, then taken out of the bag and dried in an oven at 212–217 degrees Fahrenheit, and reweighed periodically. When it stops losing weight, usually no more than twenty-four hours later, it is assumed to have zero percent moisture content. The moisture content of the original piece is calculated as:

$$M = 100 \times \frac{\text{(original or moist weight)} - \text{(oven-dry weight)}}{\text{(oven-dry weight)}}$$

I have followed this procedure in my home and found it an informative measurement method,[11] although in the early stages of drying the fumes from the wood being tested were strong. I now put the wafers for testing under a wood stove for a day to do most of the drying at a lower temperature, and finish in the oven. Wood dealers who promise "seasoned" wood should be willing to certify that the moisture content of the wood is in the optimum range. If this testing were done, the common practice of "seasoning" wood in piles of unsplit eight-foot logs would probably be abandoned.

MYTH NUMBER 5: SOME SPECIES ARE WORTH MORE THAN OTHERS

There is a story which describes a cobbler who agreed to trade a pair of boots for a pile of firewood. The woodsplitter delivered poplar (also called "popple"). A month later the boots began to come apart at the seams, and the woodsplitter returned to the cobbler to complain. The cobbler had been waiting with this reply: "What do you expect from popple boots?!"

Where I live, surrounded by hardwood trees, folks consider softwoods unworthy of the time and effort it takes to burn them. Popple, a common term for the *Populus* genus, which includes cottonwood, aspen, Balm-of-Gilead, and white poplar, is rejected. So are pine, hemlock, butternut, and basswood. And, resoundingly, elm. Walter Needham, a local old-timer, delights in telling how he was forced to burn elm once: "I had to look in the stove every so often to make sure the fire hadn't froze." But in the pine and spruce forests of Maine, they burn what they have and seem to stay alive (although our suspicion of the heating value of softwoods increases our respect for the hardiness of those lumbermen).

Concerning different heating values of different woods, popular poems compare the virtues of different species. But these poems are oversimplified, and confuse the effects of specific gravity, moisture content, and structure of the wood. For example, a commonly quoted poem ends

> Poplar gives a bitter smoke,
> Fills your eyes and makes you choke.
> Apple wood will scent your room

With an incense like perfume.
Oaken logs, if dry and old,
Keep away the winter's cold.
But ash wet or ash dry
A king shall warm his slippers by.[12]

The fact is that the fuel value of one pound of oven-dry wood is the same for all species, about 8600 BTU.[13] In general, for a given amount of warmth, the same weight of less dense poplar and the denser ash is lifted and carried for the same amount of energy. Unless firewood is bought by volume, in which case species means a great deal, the best course is to burn what is available.

Different species will dry at different rates, perhaps one reason for firemakers' preferences. Tom Gajda's data show that red oak, red maple, and white birch started with similar moisture contents and ended with similar moisture contents, but red maple got there much more quickly. Splitting and cutting to a smaller size made the drying more uniform across species.[14]

The hierarchy of fissibility of different species of hardwoods is similarly exaggerated. Factors such as type of soil, nearness to water, steepness and direction of slope where the tree grows, and, some say, phase of the moon have as much effect on wood structure as species.[15] Reaction wood from a leaning tree of any species can lead to dramatic ejections of axes or wedges. The average values for different species of tension strength perpendicular to grain direction, a laboratory measure of fissibility,[16] bear little correlation to lists of most and least fissible species found in primers on woodsmanship. The latter are based on tradition and over-generalizations from experiences with individual trees. For example, elm as a species has interlocked grain, that is, each year the direction of the vertical cells is twisted around the tree in the opposite direction from the year before. A crotch of side-hill elm with reaction wood in response to a heavy branch can be impossible to split by hand or machine. Yet a straight-grain piece of slippery elm can be as easy to split as the easiest ash. I have also encountered extremely difficult billets of ash and oak. Wood is full of surprises and should be tried out before being rejected as unsplittable or unburnable.

I am not by any means saying that all wood is the same. Each species of tree is as different from the next as cats are from dogs or mice; each individual tree, the child of sexual reproduction of its parents, has unique characteristics. As I learn to recognize these "personality" differences in the grain direction, color, texture, design, lustre, smell, and sound of woods, my experience of cutting, splitting, and burning wood is enriched. The ancient peoples closer to trees, wood, and fire had this knowledge, now all but lost. This folk wisdom can be learned in books about the personalities of trees—especially Robert Graves' awesome *White Goddess*, also Ernest Wilson's *Aristocrats of the Trees,* and the writings of George MacDonald—but as with the poem above, the books can give misleading half-truths without the renewal of fresh observation.

MYTH NUMBER 6: CHOP YOUR OWN WOOD AND IT WILL WARM YOU TWICE

This oft-quoted encouragement to the extra benefits of hard work was discovered inscribed above the mantlepiece of Henry Ford. The glib remark is obviously wrong, the sort of quip that might have impressed Henry Ford because it showed the value of hard work doing things yourself.

Though the quote over the fireplace is unattributed, its origin is probably Henry David Thoreau's *Journal* for October 22, 1853. Speaking of the fisherman, John Goodwin, preparing his own firewood and taking it home in his two-wheel handcart, Thoreau speaks of this preparation:

> . . . for it but keeps the vital heat in us that we may repeat such pleasing exercises. It warms us twice, and the first warmth is the most wholesome and memorable, compared with which the other is mere coke.

Later, in *Walden,* Thoreau says of some stumps he was working on,

> (they) warmed me twice, once while I was splitting
> them, and again when they were on the fire, so that no
> fuel could give out more heat.

The truth is, the best wood warms you ten times, each warming corresponding to a discernible step in the process: hiking up to the tree; felling it; limbing it; cutting it to billets; carrying the billets back to the house; splitting them; stacking them; then eight months later hauling them to the porch; putting them into the stove; and, finally, sitting before the fire. Some of these tasks are half-warmers, some warmers through and through, but all are best saved for quite cool weather. Drying may not proceed so rapidly in such weather but the warming of the activity itself is most enjoyed then. Calvin Coolidge was right in his highly structured farm calendar to devote January to "getting the wood in."

What would happen if we changed the adage to "Split your own wood and it will warm you ten times?" While more accurate, it does not read as nicely as Thoreau's homily, and it would probably communicate the wrong idea about the enjoyable task of woodsplitting. The notion behind the myth is basically correct.

4. *Poise and Splitting Firewood*

Miraculous power and marvelous activity—
Drawing water and hewing wood![1]

Awareness of the dynamics of one's own body can be employed
to improve one's ability at splitting, and, indeed, vice versa.
Most helpful for this understanding is the knowledge provided
in the teachings of F. Matthias Alexander. Alexander was an
actor and public lecturer at the turn of the century whose career
was interrupted by progressively worse vocal problems. Unable
to find a medical explanation or cure, he spent several years
carefully observing himself with the aid of mirrors, while speaking and at rest. Alexander discovered that just before speaking,
and even when thinking about speaking, he had been quite
unconsciously tilting his head backward while jutting his chin
forward. Though a small movement, it had cramped his neck
and cut off the column of energy in his spine and throat, stunting
his voice and presentation. At the same time, Alexander found,
he would lift his chest and narrow his back, further cramping his
larynx. After months of observation, he found that preventing
the tension and movement in his head and neck resulted in a
return of his voice as well as an improvement in his general state
of health. Asthma, which had plagued him throughout his life,
diminished gradually, until the attacks ceased altogether.

Suspecting that his discovery of the head-and-neck's role in
voice production contained even greater benefits, Alexander
proceeded in his investigation to a scrutiny of the connection of
head and neck to the entire human organism, and to the *use* of the

80

body, or more accurately the *use* of the entire self. Working from the premise of the primary importance of the head-neck relationship, he was able to teach others to become aware of their habitual *use,* thus freeing them for a re-educated use of their bodies more appropriate to the natural functioning of the human organism.[2]

The anthropologist Raymond Dart used the name "poise" for good body use, a never-fixed dynamic equilibrium that is in effect even when the body is at rest. He related poise to the balanced energies in the double spiral of voluntary muscles twisting in opposite directions through the entire length of the body.[3]

In my field tests of splitting devices, it was clear that many of the tools abused the body, destroying its poise. Not least of these was the hydraulic splitting machine, where the movement required to use the device is stoop-and-lift—a contraction—then stoop-and-lift again. In comparison, the movement with the splitting ax involves a stoop-and-lift contraction followed by a stretch skyward with ax in hand, followed by a forceful blow. Thus the overall rhythm was stoop, then stretch, then stoop, then stretch— actively moving all the time, to the benefit of the cardiovascular system.

The rhythm of this work has been preserved in some lumberjack songs, not in the ones sung in the bunkhouse, but in songs for working. An example is "The Woodsman's Alphabet," sung in 3/4 time, which provided a context for the felling or splitting movements, like someone beating time:

> A is for axes, for we all know,
> B is for boys, that can use them also,
> C is for chopping, we now do begin, . . .[4]

With the hydraulic splitting machine, I enjoyed little real exercise. A manufacturer of chainsaws and hydraulic splitters advertises its products with the testimonial from a satisfied customer: "And when I get done, I'm not even breathing hard." I find this not an advantage, but a terrible disadvantage.

THE PHASES OF SPLITTING

In splitting wood with an ax, the sequence of movements is the same with every strike of the tool, and shows minor oscillations between contraction and lengthening within the movement as a whole. These phases are illustrated in six drawings (Figure 19). The upper-most circle in the drawings represents the head-neck relationship so important to Alexander technique; it is a focal point, though not the focus, for the "primary control" of the entire body. Some associate this point more closely with the occiput at the connection between vertebra and skull, some with the hump at the bottom of the neck. The lower circle is in the vicinity of the traditional *hara;* again it is not an anatomical point but a focus of energy *(ch'i)* in use. In a simplified way, the lower circle has the energy while the upper circle directs it, although such a clear differentiation is seldom accessible to my direct experience. The lines in Figure 19 connect these centers with the earth and with the sky; the arrows suggest whether the phase of movement is contracting or lengthening. I hope it is clear that these schematics are meant to be suggestive and not prescriptive. Most interesting are the subtle variations from the generalized sequence of splitting movements which the experienced body makes to different species and structures of wood. Nonetheless, the general sequence of positions and motions in the drawings has been very helpful to those whom I have taught woodsplitting technique.

O. Set up, or preparation for work.

The body leans over, picks up the billet of wood, lifts it, sets it in place atop the splitting block, lifts the splitting ax, then steps back to the right distance for delivering the blow. There is more effort involved here than in any other phase of splitting wood; lifting and placing the wood is a chore which cannot be escaped with any special woodsplitting tool. A cord of green hardwood weighs almost two-and-a-half tons.[5] To split a twenty-pound billet into

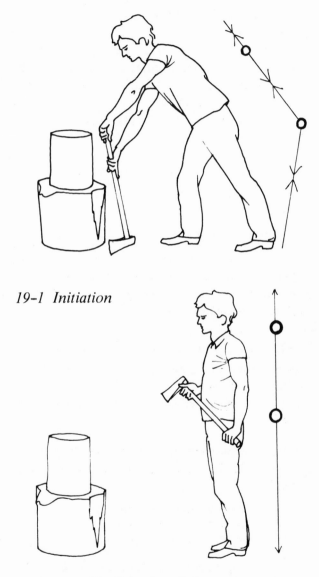

19-0 Set-up

19-1 Initiation

19. *Poise in splitting.*

eight pieces, a total of sixty pounds must be lifted just for splitting, in addition to the work of stacking before splitting and after splitting. The body contracts, particularly through the back, the muscle system which supports the shoulders and arms, and in the knees. The temptation is to contract sympathetically in the head-and-neck region, a reflex I am still learning to undo.

Eyes and hands judge how to position the billet on the splitting block so that the blow will be most effective. Such attention to the structure of the wood is especially important with round wood, since the hardest split is the first, breaking through the cohesive circle of the trunk held tight by bark. Once the circle is broken by the first split, the work is easier.

1. *Repose and initiation.*

This is the moment, protracted or brief, in which lies the greatest opportunity for centering, relaxing, undoing of tension, and lengthening. The Alexander instructions can best be used at this point, brief commands to oneself in the service of good use of the body:

a. "Let the neck free" (do not increase the tension in the neck);

b. "Let the crown of the head go forward and up" (do not pull the head back or down);

c. "Let the torso lengthen and widen out" (do not shorten and narrow the back).

This is the time for the inner preparation which makes a proper execution possible. To paraphrase an old Chinese saying from the martial arts:

> To split wood requires swiftness, but first,
>   the inner work requires slowness;
> To split wood requires strength, but first,
>   the inner work requires softness;
> To split wood requires movement, but first,
>   the inner work requires stillness.

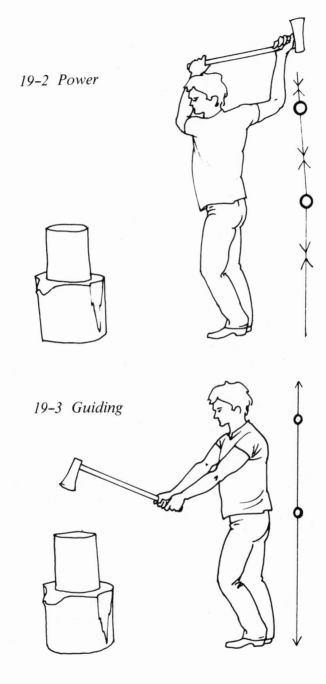

19-2 Power

19-3 Guiding

In this position, erect and relaxed, *poised,* the entire sequence of steps can be imagined. the billet of wood is seen to be split while the mind observes if the body tenses in response to the imagination. These tensions, created by anticipation, decrease the effectiveness of the stroke, and prematurely tire the body. When the tensions are perceived and relieved before they occur, it is possible to experience the splitting movement as the effortless manifestation of something which has already occurred in the mind. I let the movement happen, "as from the surface of a clear lake there leaps suddenly a fish."[6] In this way the composure of the body is not damaged. Letting the movement happen can thus be experienced not only with surprising and unforeseen events, but with deliberate and routine activities as well.

2.   *Powering the stroke.*

The splitting ax is lifted up close to the vertical axis of the body. The drawing shows but a moment in a continuous movement, the point at which the ax is highest and furthest back. Even so it is not out of balance, and the stance is not too different from one taken to lift the ax up to someone reaching for it from a second-storey window. The body is not, however, casual; the feet grip the earth strongly. Before the ax is brought to its greatest height, a series of arcs are brought into play to increase its speed toward the target. The left elbow drops abruptly to the side, then opens while the right hand slides down the handle from the head to the left hand. The major pivot point or axis is the shoulder. The elbow assists in placing the ax into the major arc originating from the shoulder. The pelvis and ankle also pivot, every axis interacting to increase or decrease the radius of the arc of the strike.

The effort of accelerating the mass of the ax head causes a contraction of the body. Deciding on the amount of power to use in the acceleration is best left to experience, that is, to the increasingly accurate judgment of how much force a particular billet will require to be split. But it is impossible to assess exactly the number of ergs of force that are necessary for the split. In

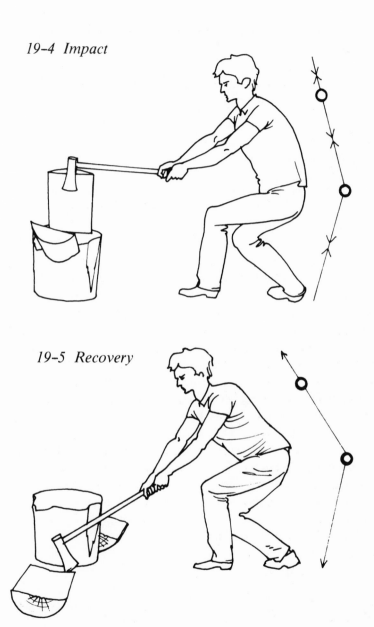

19-4 Impact

19-5 Recovery

Japanese sword fighting, which uses a similar sequence of movements, the advice is:

> Do not try to cut strongly and, of course, do not think
> of cutting weakly. You should only be concerned
> with killing the enemy.[7]

In this case the concern should be with splitting through the billet,
and not with the anticipated resistance at impact.

Compared with the rest of our sedentary lives, this moment,
when we bring down the ax, calls forth an extraordinary amount
of muscular activity, coordinated by intense concentration on all
the moving parts of the body. This is what I have been calling
contraction, without meaning the disabling tension sometimes
associated with that term. At times, such activity calls forth a
further increase of the gross motor movement, a wild thrashing of
the wood with all strength and no cunning. At these times, I pause
to recall the tale of Milo of Crotona, six times victor in wrestling at
the Olympic Games in the sixth century before Christ. He was
known for his extraordinary feats of strength, including carrying
a four-year-old heifer on his shoulders through the stadium at
Olympia, then slaying it with his fist and eating the whole of it in a
day. As Milo was passing through a forest one day, he saw the
trunk of a tree which had been partially split open by woodcutters.
He attempted to split the two halves apart with his hands, but the
woodcutters' wedge fell out and the cleft closed upon his fingers.
Trapped in this way, he was attacked and devoured by lions
(Figure 25). Taken literally or symbolically, arrogant disrespect
for the wood brings forth retribution. Remembering this tale
renews my care for the wood, and for my body in the splitting of it.
A good tool can show its power only with good use; a tool of
power used poorly, can destroy the user.

3.   *Guiding the strike.*

There is a moment, when all the accelerating power has been
delivered to the weight of the splitting ax, in which the body can

actually relax the contractions of the effort phase. The moment is brief but important. Some woodsplitters, myself included, occasionally take back a portion of the energy pushing downward in the ax head by using the handle as a lever to lift the body slightly. Since at this point the knees are bending to keep the handle perpendicular to the line of force, the experience is of taking away the supports but not falling.

This momentary loosening is the best defense against too much contraction at impact. The breath should not be held tight, but rather exhaled through this moment as well as through the point of impact. Some masters of the martial arts shout: rather than a sudden noise, it is a dramatized exhalation with a loose beginning and end. Thus, we say we "deliver a blow" to the wood.

Fine adjustments in the trajectory of the hurtling weight are made now, and it is amazing that we can hit the target exactly where we want to every time. The concentration necessary for fine adjustments, however, is susceptible to distractions, and we must learn to expect the unexpected.

4. *Impact.*

The body folds in the latter part of the stroke, to bring the ax head into its vertical descent to the wood and to prepare for the impact. The lower back is not the hinge; the folding point is where the legs meet the pelvis. The hipjoints fold back, the knees forward. The upper body remains unstressed and straight. Balance is retained. The movement is down.

This coordinated effort delivers the maximum energy when the ax helve is horizontal at impact, as is shown by the diagrams in Figure 20, based on actual measurements of available kinetic energy in the downstroke.

Measurements for Figure 20 were made just behind the ax head—the center of gravity of the ax—and at the point where the back hand grips the helve. The diagram at the left shows where these two points were in relationship to each other through the course of the stroke. The final position shown is

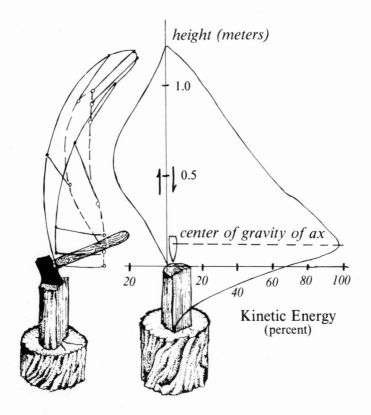

20. Kinetic energy and height of the splitting block.

below the horizontal. The diagram on the right shows the kinetic energy measured at these points both on the lift and descent as a percent of the maximum energy available in the stroke. The kinetic energy of the ax's center of gravity is greatest when the helve is horizontal at impact and decreases sharply when the wood is lower, reduced to nothing when the ax's center is 37 cm (14 inches) below the ideal point.[8] Adjustments in the height of the splitting block must be made to insure the optimum final position. For me, this is twenty inches high.

One cannot know just how all the energy put into the ax will be received when the billet of wood is hit. The problem is like that of any percussionist, though the forces are much greater in splitting. The goal is to deliver just the right amount of energy to split the billet in two, letting the ax fall gently to the block between the two halves of wood. If it splits too easily, and energy is left over, then the body can be pulled forward by the ax head; if the billet stubbornly does not split, then some of the energy at impact can be sent back up the handle as a jarring vibration. At the moment of impact, the body is intensely aware, ready to respond instantly to an abrupt and sometimes violent change in the relationship of energies between the parts of the system. The body is not tense, since that would make an unexpected bang more jarring.

The body cannot always respond quickly enough to changes that can occur on impact, such as a flying chip of wood (or of steel), or a billet which appears deceptively easy or difficult. I say "deceptively" because the woodsplitter learns to judge the type of wood he or she is dealing with and to adjust the stance of the body at this stage to accommodate the expected response of the wood to the blow. But the unexpected occurs, and here is where many people grit their teeth and tense their entire bodies. Removing or un-doing unnecessary tensions at this phase is the most difficult and requires the most conscious practice.

5. *Recovery*

In the ideal split, the moving parts are decelerated in an expected way; the weight of the ax head is neutralized and the body can lengthen again. Actually, this phase and Phase O are a combined motion of recovery and set-up for the next strike, a complicated set of movements involving setting the ax down, walking toward the split pieces, perhaps throwing one into a pile of split wood, and lifting the other onto the block.

An aid to splitting which minimizes the time taken in this

phase is suggested by Don Quigley, of the Thompson School of Applied Science at the University of New Hampshire. He recommends bolting together two discarded automobile tires through their sidewalls. As many billets as fit are placed into this cylinder atop a short splitting block, or, with some ingenuity of design, atop a taller splitting block. The split halves and quarters do not need to be set upright again. A similar aid, called a "wood jack," using a large billet scooped out in the center, was suggested by J. J. Thomas' *Illustrated Annual Register of Rural Affairs for 1873.*

What is illustrated in Figure 19–5 is not the ideal case—the ax has been thrown to the side and off the block. This emergency requires even greater trust in the lengthening of the body, rather than a compensatory contraction. If the body tries to pull the ax, the pressure on the lower back is very great and may strain it. Better to fall forward than seriously wrench the back. Best to simply collapse further at the hipjoints and knees, following the downward movement.

Some woodsplitters whom I encounter curse the wood and the oil companies, the tool, and their aim, but they continue to work at it every weekend. Yet when they split wood, I observe them to pause at this phase, when the split billet lies before them, while their eyes quickly study the inner faces of the cleft wood, exposed for the first time to the light of day. I, too, pause here to gaze at this revealed stuff of Nature, perhaps for the same reason:

> Raise the stone and there thou shalt find Me,
> Cleave the wood and there am I.[9]

Though perhaps unconsciously stored beneath worldly concerns with the energy crisis and so forth, I think this curiosity to see what lies within the wood and awe at what I find there are part of the reason that I and others continue to split wood.

The emphasis in this formulation of expansion and contraction in the motions of woodsplitting is on the recovery, the poise from which the efforts go out and to which the body returns. The Christian notion of longing for God has a similar meaning in the lengthening of the body. The task to be done calls forth the contraction; the expectation in splitting wood is that one will get a good workout, thus gaining healthy exercise while gaining heating fuel. The popular view is expressed by Dr. Johnson:

> How much happiness is gained, and how much misery escaped, by frequent and violent agitation of the body.[10]

But a tense and cramped body works less well than a poised body. The woodsplitter is rewarded by the extra mental effort to recuperate and lengthen again.

MOVING WOOD

> The children stagger under loads of wood.
> —*Lamentations*, 5:13

The most difficult part about firewood—felling, splitting, or burning—is lifting and moving it. A cord of green hardwood weighs nearly five thousand pounds, some green billets weighing well over fifty pounds. Dudley Cook estimates that twenty-four tons must be lifted from felling with an ax to feeding the fire for every cord of firewood.[11] These weights and these work loads—foot-pounds per minute or rate of lifting or how much wood *can* a woodchuck chuck—approach the limits of the average healthy male and female found by biomechanical measurements.[12] There are several tools and techniques to assist the movement of such a mass.

Many of the great religious traditions caution us to keep our hands free unless they are actually being used, that is, don't carry anything in the hand. In Don Juan's instructions to Carlos Castenada, the purpose of freeing the hands is to open them to interchanges of energy with natural forces, the same sort of energy exchange that I have spoken of with the ax and the wood.

A good physiological reason for keeping the hands free when carrying is the frailty of the arms and shoulders for supporting weights. The only connection of the bones of the arms and shoulders to the structure of the rest of the body is a weak joint between the clavicle and sternum at the top of the chest. The shoulders actually float between layers of muscle. Thus the arms are strong and flexible, but lack direct support from the earth through the bones. Carrying heavy things, including axes and firewood, can hurt the tone of the muscles in which the shoulders rest. The shoulders can also be pulled down or bent lopsided.

Any heavy weight needs to be supported by the bony framework directly over the body's center of gravity (the lower circles in Figure 19) in such a way that the spine is not bent. Several examples are shown in Figure 21 (as well as the ax sling in Figure 11). When the billet is on the shoulder, it is best not oriented front and back, but turned out at a diagonal to the line of travel, so its weight is as close to the backbone as possible. When carrying wood up high, it is best to keep in mind the image of a shepherd carrying a sheep, the load wrapped around the neck, the cushioned weight centered directly over the center of gravity atop an erect spine, two hooves in each hand to steady the load. If the arms are called into service it is to balance a load or to hold the load close to the center of gravity (as in the two-person timber carrier). Carrying wood in a pack basket (Figure 21) or lashed to a backpack frame are other good methods of balancing the load and not straining the shoulder. It should be clear from this that the popular canvas or leather wrap-around firewood carrier is not a good way to carry a heavy weight; with this method, or with wood carried in the arms, many trips are much preferred. I remember, and regret, telling my brother to "stack me up" with wood, crumpling my spine to balance the weight.

While the average household does not now burn the twenty to fifty cords of wood once required each winter by the fireplaces of a New England farmhouse, transporting a few cords from forest to woodshed to fire requires a better method than that offered by the wood-carriers described above. The boom in sales of small trucks, jeeps, and garden carts is related to this need. The cart in Figure 21

back-pack basket   *canvas carrier*

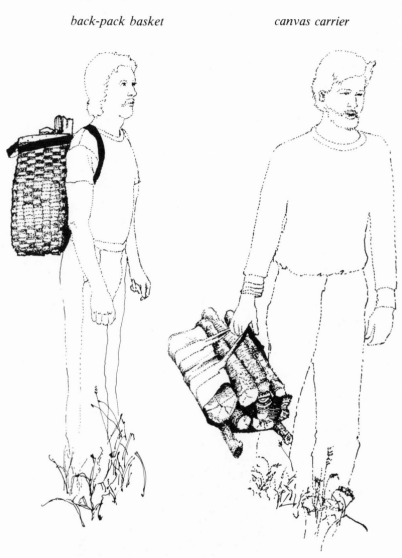

21. Moving wood.

timber carrier

cant-dog (or Peavey)

*handcart, front
gate removed
for dumping*

has a welded steel frame with gates at both ends so that the contents may be dumped without turning the cart upside-down. The carter (the person who pulls it) arranges the load to rest over the wheel axles, which leaves little weight to lift except when ascending steep hills. With two parallel shafts for handles, the carter can move forward or back to keep the burden at the body's center of gravity. Using both arms hanging straight down does not strain them; for very large loads, a strap can be run over one shoulder and across the chest and attached to the bottom of the front of the cart.

Moving heavy billets or logs short distances can be done with the leverage of a cant-dog or cant-hook, named differently and often confusedly for the hardware these tools have at their ends. The Peavey is a cant-dog with a straight pike point at the end of the shaft, manufactured by Joe Peavey, a Maine lumberman, beginning in 1858, but is not a new type of cant-dog and is not the descriptive name for every tool of this type.[13] A Timber Jack is a cant-dog with a strut welded to its base, which can lift a large log off the ground for safer cutting. The unadorned cant-dog, however, can do the same thing by lifting the log onto a stick of wood, and is much more versatile without the strut.

REFINEMENTS IN MOVEMENT

Suggestions for refining lifting and splitting techniques cannot be found in books except as metaphor. For example,

> The motion should be rooted in the feet,
> released through the legs,
> controlled by the waist,
> and manifested through the fingers.[14]

At first glance, this seems simple: our society places too much emphasis on the muscles of the arms and hands, when analysis of a complete technique, as in this chapter, shows that the hip joints ("waist") determine the balance and power of the splitting stroke. Figure 22 shows well the sinuous movement of the body in which

22. *Reaching up to maximize the stroke.*

the waist and legs lead the strike and the ax follows. Though felling a tree, the similarity to the high strokes used with the early stone axes, and thus to splitting, makes this painting appropriate in this context. It is obvious that this woodsman must lead to his right with his hips, drop his right foot in readiness to receive the majority of his weight, and follow with the arms, fingers, and ax. But the saying from Ta'i Chi Ch'uan above is more complex than these observations can penetrate, and further study requires a teacher—Alexander, martial arts, or someone who splits wood well—who will watch and guide you to better use of your body.

5. The Wood

Stranger, if thou hast learned a truth which needs
No school of long experience, that the world
Is full of guilt and misery, and hast seen
Enough of all its sorrows, crimes, and cares,
To tire thee of it, enter this wild wood
And view the haunts of Nature.
                    —William Cullen Bryant
                    "Inscription for the Entrance
                    to a Wood," 1825

From the hundreds of myths and legends about wood known in ancient and modern times, it is clear that forest, tree, billet, stick, fire, smoke, and ash—which I refer to collectively as The Wood—are, each in its own way, suffused with spirit. This spirit is not bound by the same constraints of time and space as appear to bind us. Its power is vaguely and unknowingly invoked by such common superstitions as "knock on wood." Where does the power of this unknown spirit of The Wood originate? In Bruno Bettelheim's analysis of fairy tales, *The Uses of Enchantment,* the spirit is seen as a projection onto The Wood of the great unknown of our own unconscious mind:

> The forest . . . symbolizes the place in which inner
> darkness is confronted and worked through; where
> uncertainty is resolved about who one is; and where
> one begins to understand who one wants to be. [1]

Yet in the animistic context of the Findhorn Community, an experimental agricultural and spiritual community in Scot-

land, and its like, the same power is perceived to be inde-
pendent of us, and to be controlled by elemental and other
spiritual beings which dwell within and are identified with
The Wood itself.[2] Is a reverence for The Wood a primitive
superstition, or a wise and proper respect for the earthly
divinities which care for the realms of Nature? Certainly
those who know wood intimately in a scientific sense
express their awe of it, even if they are not specific about its
source: Bruce Hoadley's *Understanding Wood* and Eric Sloane's
A Reverence for Wood are recent examples.

In my own experience, both the sacred and the profane
points of view about The Wood are true, yet it is an impossible task (at which one must nonetheless never give up) to
differentiate with certainty phenomena belonging to the
spiritual and to the material aspects of The Wood. The
stories and legends about The Wood help in this task of
differentiation, and are compelling in their familiarity and
"rightness." The stuff of these stories—myth in the best
sense—is not from the practical Age of Men, but from the
Age of Heroes and Gods, a once-upon-a-time that yet lurks
in the background of our thought and experience. Sir James
George Frazer's *The Magic Art,* and Robert Graves' *The White
Goddess,* are packed with the lore of The Wood in its different
forms. Are these myths true, in a practical, scientifically
verifiable sense? No, not at first, perhaps never; but on
another level they are as true, if not more true, than the
banalities of everyday life. Through much of *Homo sapiens'*
existence, the mythic has been felt to be more true than the
idiosyncracies of time and individual history, because its
truth transcends variation and reaffirms the original plan of
creation.[3]

I leave first-hand observation of The Wood in all its forms
to the reader, but I wish to present here some of the relevant
myths and other stories briefly, so that the experience of
rediscovery will be the richer.

Stories about The Wood take place in three discernible ritual centers: 1.) *felling,* oriented to the ritual center of the living tree; 2.) *burning,* oriented to the ritual center of the hearth-fire; and, 3.) between the two, *splitting,* at the ritual center of the woodyard.

TREE

I am the shade screening you from the summer sun. My fruits and restoring drinks quench your thirst as you journey onward. I am the beam that holds your house; the door of your homestead; the bed on which you lie; and the timber that builds your boat. I am the handle of your hoe, the wood of your cradle, and the shell of your coffin.[4]

Trees are the largest and oldest terrestrial living things we know. Dwarfed by the ancient giants, men have felt challenged, and have alternated between companionship with and hostility against trees. Many adventure stories take place in the forest, where the relationship of men and trees must be worked out, though it is seldom recognized that the forest per se is the hero's adversary. More often, the hero encounters the many beings spawned and sheltered by the forest—faun, bacchant, satyress, ogress, nymph, naiad, dryad, menad, gnome, gorgon, babiaga.[5] All of these, nevertheless, are beings that represent the spirits of the trees and forest, or The Wood.

Although the hero may have entered the forest for practical reasons—to treat with The Wood in its material aspect[6]—his predicament in the forest requires a knowledge of the sacred side of trees. *Tree* comes from the Indo–European root **deru-**, as do the words *Druid* (knower of trees, name of the cult of woodsmen priests), *dryad* (the elemental being who inhabits and represents a tree), *true, truth, trust,* and *durable.* Our language is clear and consistent on the deepest meaning for us of trees.

In Chinese philosophy, wood is the basic element of spring-time, the first of The Five Dynamic Physical Forces, along with fire, soil, metal, and water. [7] In Western tradition, the three basic sources of the maternal, that is, contexts for experiencing intimacy with Mother Nature, are earth, water, and wood. [8] Matrix, matter, and mother are fundamentally equivalent. They give support, as the ground we stand on, and a frame of reference for understanding all that surrounds us. An image from a fourteenth-century treatise of philosophy shows the prototypical tree sprouting from Adam, the prototypical living being (Figure 23). This is the Gnostic Adam, not as the lucky fellow who played in a bountiful garden, but as the first being, the living stuff from which all else was made, and thus neither masculine nor feminine. This stuff is called by the alchemical philosophers *prima materia,* or original matter. The arrow is from Mercurius/Hermes, god of lightning (as in the thunderstone, cf. Chapter 2) and of the snake (as in the poised spine, cf. Chapter 4); he is the enlivening aspect who awakes the sleeping *prima materia.* The tree is the result.

In a Nordic myth, God created men by breathing life into wood, the reverse of the order of creation shown in Figure 23. [9] Co-incidentally created, The Wood is endowed with the mystical power of human events which take place close by. A good example comes from modern Portugal:

> The phenomenon of Fàtima began on the thirteenth of May in a sere pasture where Lucia dos Santo, ten, and her cousins, Francisco and Jacinta Marto, nine and seven, grazed their flocks. A beautiful woman 'more brilliant than the sun' appeared above a small oak. . . . The tiny Chapel of the Apparitions stands in place of the oak, long ago (that tree was) stripped for relics. [10]

Christ is often identified with the Cross, and early Christians believed that Christ's Cross was made from the Tree of

23. The tree grows from Adam as prima materia.

Knowledge of Good and Evil. The living Christ is symbolized by his crucifixion on a living tree. So too, Odin hung in
the World Tree, Yggdrasil, for nine days to attain his
supreme wisdom and power. [11]

In ancient times, every center of habitation had a sacred
grove nearby, a center of religious ritual, a temple with
living pillars. Sir James George Frazer's entire thirteen-
volume study, *The Golden Bough*, was devoted to the discovery
of the reason that a man who guarded the grove at Nemi, in
the Italian Piedmont, could at any time be challenged to
mortal combat; if the guard was killed, the victor succeeded
him as guard. Frazer found that the guard was a priest who
had become, through his position, the consort of the goddess of The Wood, and thus himself a divinity. The goddess
had many names, often Diana, and her territory was the
circle of a sacred grove, an entire forest, or a single tree.

Because of the sacred nature of the tree, felling has been
approached in a ritual manner; the feller moves around the
base of the tree first with ritual phrases, then with cutting
tools. The world round, woodsmen have spoken to trees
before felling them, to tell of their intended use. For a tree
not thus spoken to, "no ax would cut it down, nothing would
injure it, for there would be no purpose for which it might be
used." [12]

FIRE

It warms the house and cooks the food, but if it
has reason to be angered, it jumps from the fireplace and burns up the house and the village. [13]

Historians of ancient religions agree that before man articu-
lated calendars in reverence of the sun and moon, "he feared
and cultivated fire, a housefriend as well as a destructive
force." [14] The control of fire is a distinctly human experience.
Next to the sun, fire is the most intense energy transforma-
tion we commonly observe. Our species has been building

fires and gazing into their changing colors for some two million years, and it would not surprise me to discover that we have a physical relationship to the feeling and sight of fire. Count Rumford's innovation of enclosing the hearth-fire in a cast iron stove is 200 years old, and has been proven a more efficient use of wood energy for heating than an open fireplace. Yet people continue to include energy-inefficient fireplaces in their homes. [15] An extreme example is a recent President of the United States who installed an especially large fireplace and an especially large air conditioner in his Florida home so that he could watch the flames without becoming overheated. Though the incongruity in this case is pathetically funny, it shows that the effect of direct experience of the heat and light that the fireplace allows should not be ignored. Experiments have proven the healthful benefits of exposure to the full spectrum of sunlight, and the degenerating effects of blocking part of this spectrum (with the use of sunglasses, artificial lighting, most window glass, etc.). [16] A similar, more subtle effect might well be discovered with firelight.

Fire consumes the *prima materia* that has been prepared for burning, and sends it back to heaven. The symbolism of fire is celestial, a form of the mystic light. The ascetic Christian monks of the desert cultivated the presence of this inner sacred light until they became like fire. For example, "Once Abba Joseph stretched his hands towards Heaven and his fingers became like two flames of fire. Then, turning to one of the monks, he said: 'If you wish, you may become entirely like fire!'" [17]

Different types of fire are appropriate in different contexts. Hephaistos' roaring industrial fires for the forging of the ax are quite different from the gentle fire tended by the goddess of the hearth, Hestia (or Vesta, both meaning hearth or center). The hearth is the center of the home (*focus* is the Latin word for hearth) and integrates the household

24. Cooking fire as hearth.

into an intimate harmony. Home fires kindle our inner warmth, arouse our hearts, our individual centers. The fire on the hearth consumes wood to warm our bodies or partly consumes food which our bodies finish consuming. Fire in the latter aspect, the cooking fire, performs the essential act of culture, transforming raw matter into edible food. [18]

The hearth is in many traditions arranged like the cross (or tree) set horizontally, the intersection of the two pieces at the center, and four stones set at the edge of the hearth circle at the compass points. The fire is started with male and female "fire-sticks" heated by rubbing. Likewise, the pieces of wood separated in preparation for burning are re-united at the center of the hearth-cross.

Several of the many rituals that surround the building, lighting, and tending of a fire have been passed down to this day. Disguised as "practical advice," these instructions lack only the invocation to Hestia, and the feeling of her guidance. Frustrated by homes without hearths, many people find Hestia's intimate circle elswhere, around barbecues and campfires, gladly performing the unique rituals appropriate to these fires.

The ritual circle of felling in the fist realm and the ritual circle of burning in the third realm must be kept separate; when the two are improperly mixed, the result can be dangerous or regressive. For example, according to primitive South American cultures, the mythic food of Man before he possessed fire was rotten wood.[19] In this crude early state, eating, which should be Hestia's domain, is confused with harvesting trees. Fire separates the realms in cooking. Fire must have its limits also, forest fire being the most terrible mixing of realms.

BILLET

Splitting takes place neither in the forest nor on the hearth, but in its own ritual center, a woodyard with splitting block in the center. Splitting firewood as we know it depends on neatly sawn surfaces at top and bottom, and thus has been practiced only as long as there have been saws, that is, only the last six thousand years. Bucking wood with an ax into billets, and opening the billets along the grain to make smaller pieces, has been practiced since there have been hafted axes, additional thousands of years. Splitting wood has associations which go right back to the origins of man, to the basic experiences of wood, tools, and fire. Fire for warmth, cooking, and protection grows larger more quickly with wood of smaller girth. Splitting essentially makes the cut tree readier for the transformations of the fire.

Billet is from the Latin *billa* for small log, and, earlier, from the name of the White Goddess of Nature of the Sumerians, Belili. A modern French use of the old word is dimly related—a love letter is sometimes called a *billet doux,* literally a sweet billet of perfumed parchment which must be slit (split) open to reveal its contents.

The spirit, or Goddess Belili, is within The Wood, particularly as a short round. For this reason, at the center of all ceremonial fires for important events is an unsplit billet. At the midwinter solstice, for example, when the day is shortest, the unsplit yule log is brought in to banish darkness and return the warmth and light of summer. Likewise, native drummers from around the world find a tree from which to fashion a drum, invoke the spirit of the tree, fell the tree, and hollow and cover an unsplit billet to produce the drum. Each playing of the drum evokes the spirit still within the unsplit wood.

We must not confuse splitting with the other realms or ritual centers associated with The Wood. Splitting is inappropriate to the realm of the hearth: the Mongols think it a sin to cleave wood near a fire, or to put an ax into the fire. [20] A tree's splitting during felling is one of the most dangerous accidents that can occur. A tree, cut through part way, can suddenly split apart from the bottom up, as if struck by lightning at the base, the severed part lashing about on the springy hinge of the unsevered part. Such a tree gone wild is sometimes called a "barber's chair," because it can knock the feller up into the air; the free part of the tree can also travel sideways, as it did toward Old Henry ("Felling," Chapter 2), killing him. [21]

Naming the divinity of the realm of splitting firewood is quite complicated since in this realm the human splitter is most prominent. As The Wood is split, no roots vanish into the earthly matrix and no heat, light, or smoke vanishes into the heavens. The parts of the ritual of splitting are simply human, ax, block, and billets. We need to look further to discover the essence of splitting.

TRANSGRESSION

A recurrent theme of the myths and legends about The Wood is that we must come to an understanding with these powers when in their domain . . . or else! To illustrate this notion, I will tell a story, told on the Greek island of Cos at the turn of the century, that is important for its thorough expression of this theme. A young prince thinks the spirits of a sacred grove of trees have assisted in the sudden accidental (though just) death of his cruel father.

> Filled with the powers of revenge, the prince, now king, set off with his axmen to lay low the sacred trees and offending spirits. All went speedily at first as they fell flat the tall trees one after another. Their youthful vigor was slackened, however, by a huge oak in the center of the grove that seemed to resist each blow. Using their sharp axes with all their strength, they had cut nearly half through the mighty tree when they heard a plaintive cry from the heart of the oak. The axmen were ready to drop their axes and flee when the king shouted to them, "Smite it again, you dogs, pay no heed to spirits!" And because their fear of him was greater, they took their axes to the tree and dealt still more telling blows. Then, upon (the woodcutters') reaching the very center, a mighty gush of blood jetted forth, and a voice cried: "Oh, ye who fear not God!" As the tree trembled, and swayed, and finally crashed to the ground, the voice was heard again: "Even as God

has punished your father, even so and three times
worse will he punish you." From the direction of the
voice there appeared a young woman's head, her
hair disheveled and drenched with the blood of the
tree, which now filled the ground on which they
stood. The youths were seized with terror and ran,
but the king turned on the female spirit like a mad-
man and raised his sword and brought it down on
her with all his strength. But when he tried to with-
draw his sword, he could not; for in his blind anger,
he had missed her and wedged it deep within the tree
stump. Without his weapon he too was gripped with
fear and fled to his palace and took to his bed. That
night, as he slept, he saw a dream. A fairy came to
him and took him forcefully by the hand and led him
to the place where the trees had been cut down.
"Stay and behold what you have done," she said. As
he looked, he saw each felled tree become a flame,
and in an instant there were fires all around him
burning furiously, singeing his hair and licking at his
feet. He was powerless to flee, as the fires united into
a single holocaust that seemed bent on destroying
him completely. As the tongues of flame leaped to
mid-heaven, he saw there the fairy pointing at him
and saying, "This and much worse is the lot of those
who destroy my beautiful trees." As she faded, a
terrible cold wind blew through the fire-ravaged
place as if all the north winds of the earth had united
against him. The king began to shiver and his ulcer-
ous fire wounds broke into dry cracks to the very
bone, and with each shake of his body they stretched
and slackened, bringing him wracking pain and terrible anguish.

As he stood helpless and afraid, an old woman
approached him. She was hunch-backed, horrid,
filthy, and scabby—a terrible figure. She came right
up to the king and with her bony and decrepit hand
reached out for his sword, still lodged in the tree
trunk. Without strain or difficulty, she snatched it
free from its bond and raised it to her ghastly face.
Like a priest performing a ritual, she breathed upon

it three times, each time filling the blade with viru-
lent seeds from her poisonous breath. "I am the
Ravening Hunger," she intoned in a voice filled with
hate and prophecy. As the king opened his mouth in
fright, she raised herself high and plunged the sword
into his gaping mouth and down into his belly, and
as she drew it out, all the seeds of the ravening
hunger planted themselves in his entrails. So imme-
diate was the effect that he strained to lick the blood
from the sword as it was withdrawn from his mouth.
An overpowering and insatiable hunger and thirst
came over him. Cisterns and wells he drank, full
rivers and lakes, but nothing could sate his awful
hunger. So great was his distress and overpowering
his need, that he awoke from his dream.

"I am hungry," were his first words. The palace
servants made ready all the foods of the realm but
the king's ravenous hunger knew no bounds. In
short time, he had consumed all the food of the land
and waters of the realm. Still he hungered and thirsted
for more. There was nothing left to sell for food,
nothing but a son and daughter. When he could find
no buyer for his daughter, he tried to eat her. But the
king's desperate plan was thwarted by her brother,
and the two children fled for their lives. Now totally
alone, without family, without friends, without servants, and [with] only an empty kingdom, the king
began to tear at his own flesh, gnawing it greedily
with his teeth until he had devoured himself to
death.

This ghastly story is important because it includes many
elements found scattered in other stories about relationships to
The Wood, and thus affords a context for understanding these
elements. The three realms of felling, splitting, and burning, with
their attendant rituals, have been badly confused and violated in
the story, although it is the attempted splitting of the female
spirit on the tree stump that brings the specific revenge of
ravening hunger.

We can compare the story of Milo (Figure 25): Milo's arrogance against the natural order finally meets a greater power. His hand is clasped by the split wood and, like the young king, he is devoured (though by lions). The punishment of Old Henry, quoted in the section on felling trees, is for a similar trangression. Dare we include the two thousand or more cases every year of mangled and severed fingers from hydraulic woodsplitting machines as lack of respect for The Wood?[22]

In a like spirit of respect, nineteenth-century writers and artists warned of the consequences of ravaging Nature in pursuit of Progress. Their image of Man's destruction was the ax and the tree stump, which figured prominently in the paintings of the Hudson River school of artists. The passage at the beginning of the section on felling trees was written by an author of this

25. Milo of Crotona stuck in the cleft.

group. The threatened revenge was "that barrenness of mind, that sterile desolation of the soul, in which sensibility to the beauty of nature cannot take root." [23] There are other retribu- tions, as well. The psychologist Russell Lockhart finds in the fate of the young king of Cos a perfect illustration of what he sees in his terminal cancer patients. They have refused to recognize the existence of the Spirit, the Other Reality, in their world and in themselves, and the Other has shown its power by causing them to consume themselves. [24]

Paul Bunyan. Why has Paul Bunyan, the great lumberjack, evaded these retributions? He showed complete disregard for the spirit in trees, knocking them down by the hundreds, in one story even tearing one up by the roots each morning to comb his beard. The reason Paul Bunyan has avoided The Wood's retri- bution is that he is not a man, but a god, and not a god of the forest, but of the ax. His attitude distills the cut-and-split virtue of the ax. Paul Bunyan is the confused, spontaneous American recreation of the classical god Saturn, or Cronos, father of Zeus. Saturn, too, was a Titan, who brought agriculture and its tools to mankind, just as huge Paul Bunyan taught men how to cut and split trees and invented all the tools necessary for the task. Saturn is often pictured in Greece and Rome with a scythe, which for the ancient Mediterranean was the cutting instrument of importance. In much of America, the sort of vegetation confronted by the early settlers was forest, and the ax, not the scythe, was the first implement of agriculture. For big Paul Bunyan, the trees were as grass, and his tree-felling actions were often compared to those of a scythe-user.

To my knowledge, the only time that Paul Bunyan en- countered any trouble from The Wood was when guiding a ground-breaking plow over logged-off land. (Recall that the early uses of the ax included cultivation to clear away tree roots and break up the soil, so plowing should not be considered incongruous with the use of the ax.) Paul split through the center of a huge cedar stump with the plow, and it clamped together again on his pants. His workmen had to hitch twenty teams of oxen to the stump to pull it out by the roots. The similarity to Milo's encounter is obvious, but it seems important that in Paul's case, the final escape from the stump is never fully explained.

When men entered the American wilderness, the power of The Wood was overwelming. Paul Bunyan—the ax— overwhelmed the forest, establishing a sort of rough-hewn balance between Man and Nature. He was finally defeated by "the women things" who gently domesticated his work- men, tempering their methods and grandiosity. Perplexed, Paul moved off to his logging camp deep in the forest.[25] His spirit is still invoked, sometimes with too much enthusiasm, by the names of woodsplitting tools: Monster Maul, Wood- butcher, and others in Chapter 2.

DISMEMBERMENT

In the realm of humans, arrogance to The Wood is always punished. On a mystic level, the dismemberment of the young king of Cos, of Milo, and of Old Henry has a positive side, however. Many religions have rejoiced in the resurrec- tion and renewal of their vegetable gods who have been torn apart at harvest time. A modern example comes from the English songs about John Barleycorn and his torture and apparent death at the hands of the reapers:

> They hired men with the scythes so sharp
> To cut him off at the knee,
> They rolled him and tied him by the waist,
> And served him most barbarously.
> They hired men with the sharp pitchforks
> Who pricked him to the heart,
> And the loader he served him worse than that,
> For he bound him to the cart.

> They wheeled him round and round the field
> Till they came unto a barn,
> And there they made a solemn mow
> Of poor John Barleycorn.
> They hired men with the crab-tree sticks
> To cut him skin from bone,
> And the miller he served him worse than that,
> For he ground him between two stones.[26]

The marvel is that the part of John Barleycorn that is not ground into meal is up and sprouting again the next spring; the part that is ground serves to renew the workmen, as porridge or beer. Another example of dismemberment and renewal is Jesus, whose body, in the form of bread, was broken before it was eaten, renewing the eater. Also, in dreams or visions, apprentice shamans or wizards witness their own dismemberment by demons who then put the pieces back together, this time better.[27]

In these stories emphasizing resurrection, the dismemberment is approached in a ritual manner, and the participants are aware of the sacred materials with which they are working. The acts of cutting, splitting, and burning are known to have repercussions, and these repercussions are anticipated. For those who suffer from these repercussions, such as Lockhart's cancer patients, the opportunity exists to see how the divinities of the three realms have been ignored and confused, and perhaps to reverse the process to a fuller life.

Cleaving is a kind of dismembering, cutting with but not against the grain, requiring a surgeon's discernment for placement of the division. Recall the Chinese cook who did not cut but rather separated a carcass of meat, leaving his knife as sharp as it began. Splitting at its best gives the feeling that the two split halves have been coaxed, not bludgeoned, apart.

A decisive but well-placed split readies the material for the final stage of burning. Thus, from an ancient Hebrew *midrash:* "Adam and Eve were made back to back, joined at the shoulders; then God split them with an ax stroke, cutting them in two." [28] In the *Symposium,* Plato similarly postulated that men and women were first formed as four-armed, four-legged androgynous pairs, who were then split. He went on to state what was implicit in the *midrash:* our task is to return to our true mate, but front-to-front, with eyes open, in a sacred marriage in which the original unity is recreated at a higher level. C. G. Jung has postulated the very same process in the separation of the male and female aspects of one's psyche, which is to be followed by a reintegration of these halves, each more matured through experience, in a *mysterium coniunctionis,* or mystical marriage. [29] The symbolically hopeful ending to the story of the young king of Cos is the escape of his son and daughter, giving fresh male and female energies with the potential for reintegration with The Wood at some point in the future. So too, many myths of creation picture the original One, the undifferentiated totality which has been expertly split into halves or quarters to create the world. [30] Our task, in the terms of these myths, is to return to the One, remaking it *greater* through our awareness of it. These re-unions and marriages take place in the third and final realm of fire, and are always symbolized by flames or brilliant light. But such transcendent experiences require correct preparation in the realm of separation or splitting:

> For nothing can be sole or whole
> That has not been rent. [31]

The refined fire of the sacred marriage can, of course, be demeaned to the temporary pleasure of sexual intercourse. At the local sawmill, where skill means doing what splitting does, namely sawing with the grain of the wood, the men have a large color poster on the wall of a naked woman lying on her back, propped up on her elbows, with knees bent and legs spread apart, an erotic version of the birth position. As the luminous and perfumy sawn surfaces of the new boards pass through their hands, the sawmill workers exchange lewd jokes. Though they do not seem to realize it, they are being aroused by The Wood, but they are expressing their excitement in a narrow way. This prevents them from a richer, conscious experience of The Wood, and also excludes women from the company of sawyers. Women are, however, not excluded from the more refined fire of the *mysterium coniunctionis,* nor for that matter from the mythic level of the experience of splitting firewood.

THE CLEFT

Dismembering is the mystic significance of the splitting; the cleft is its central feature. As we have already seen, the open cleft is a source of energy, and is often used as a symbol for energy in art, as in the knot-hole in Adam's tree (Figure 23).The French psychologist Nadine Suares has found that, when you ask some-one to draw a tree, if the drawn tree has a cleft or knot-hole in the side, perhaps with an owl or chipmunk peeping out, then there is a lively spirit and an excitement of discovery in that person.

When embodied in myth, the spirit that exits from the cleft Wood is often a spirit of air or fire. Animals or humans who are trapped, then liberated from trees, stumps, or billets are affected by the experience by flying or a feeling of lightness.[32] Ariel, released from his entrapment in a tree by Prospero's artful splitting of it, went on to play the tricks of air and fire in *The Tempest.* The young king of Cos, above, releases a spirit of fire when he splits the stump with his sword. The Malekula tribes-men of the New Hebrides Islands elicit this power of the cleft by splitting part way their long drums, called slit gongs, and hollow-ing out the drum through this split. They strike the gong near the split to invoke the ancestral voices (see figure 26).[33]

Birth is associated with a cleft that opens, emits an energy, then closes again. We all share birth from a cleft in the mother's womb. The Lapps traditionally symbolized the birth deity, Sarakka, by a partly split piece of wood, and the father split firewood during the mother's labor.[34] Ovid records the tale of a pregnant mother turned into a tree; the child is born through a cleft in the tree.[35] A cure for ailing children that has survived almost to the present has been to split a small living tree from the base upwards six feet or so, pull the two halves apart, pass the suffering child through, then close and bind the cleft. If the cleft heals, the sufferer will be cured, in effect reborn. [36]

Instead of finding the supporting matrix of the providing earthly mother, symbolized by the healing power of cleft wood, an arrogant attitude toward The Wood arouses the devouring or vengeful mother, also sometimes associated with cleft or split wood—indeed, reaction wood in its deepest sense.

26. The ten-foot-tall mother-gong of the Malekula.

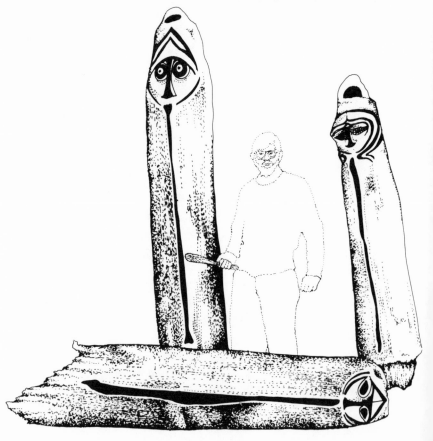

Instead of feeding, she brings hunger; instead of supporting, she entraps. Franz Boas collected many versions of the following tale showing the hazards of the cleft for an arrogant young man among the natives of the American Northwest:

> A youth is told to split wood. It is made hard by magic, then suddenly soft, so that the wedges drop out into the crack. The youth is told to get them, and the people cause the crack to close. He spits out red paint [to simulate blood], puts his "thunder-stone" [ax] across, and is saved. When the people are gone, he splits the wood and carries it home, when it assumes a large bulk. [37]

This magic wood turns hard, then soft, then opens, then closes, then becomes light, then bulky! How like splitting firewood! For young men in this culture, caution is necessary at every step.

A supposedly true story claimed by the historians of a dozen of the United States tell of a pioneer who is splitting a log for fence rails when a number of Indians surprise and capture him. The pioneer says he will come with them, presumably to be tortured, but asks the Indians to wait until he has finished splitting the log. They agree, thinking the proposal funny. Then the splitter asks them to help pull the log apart by putting their hands in the crevice held open by a splitting wedge. The Indians do so. The pioneer quickly knocks the wedge out, catching their fingers in the crevice, and kills them all with his ax. [38] That this story is claimed by so many different localities, and in slightly different versions, shows to me the attraction of this metaphor of getting caught in the cleft. It is not as tidy a story mythologically as the others, but does fit in with the older legends of The Wood, in that the Indians' violence and lack of caution meets with a vengeful backlash.

REMEMBERING

Splitting firewood is dismembering it, but to avoid the vengeful mother, I need to *re*member. Learning about how other people at other times propitiated the earth deities is useful for this, but is not enough. Men and women of today must rediscover this connection between themselves and ancient usages through first-hand experience. The unwritten saying of Jesus quoted before has been helpful to me in this work of remembering. I shall quote it in full, and then look at it more closely to pull together the themes of splitting presented in different places in this book:

> Jesus saith, Wherever there are two, they are not without God.
> And wherever there is one alone, I say, I am with him.
> Raise the stone, and there thou shalt find Me.
> Cleave the wood and there am I. [39]

One and two: Why is there the prologue about one and two, when it seems that neither is favored or rejected? I approach the single billet, round, a symbol of wholeness, showing the entire life of the tree. As a whole, as one thing, it is complete unto itself and therefore beyond the world of rela-tionships. When I split the billet, I at once double it and halve it. By dividing the one thing, I bring it into material existence—now there are two sticks of wood where before there were no sticks—and I expose its inner polarity and symmetry. But each half becomes a new unity, a single stick, which may be split further. The two become many, the many become a woodpile, which is a unity again. *Split* has the same root word as do *splint* and *splice*. Likewise, *cleave* has a double meaning: to separate and to attach (to). This oscillation between one and two exists also with the relationship of my body to the wood in splitting: at first the connection is made with the wood, as my energy expands to meet it. Then that connection, as well, is split.

The one billet becomes the two sticks. The tension of these symmetrical opposites brings in the third, which is the splitter. But three readily spawn the fourth, which is the image of wholeness or completion—that is, the I or Me discovered in the process. I was amazed to discover a similar axiom in the writings of the alchemist Maria Prophetissa: "Out of the One

comes Two, out of Two comes Three, and from the Third
comes the One as the Fourth."[40]

Raise the stone: This, I have discovered, means "lift the
ax." Archeologists have shown that metals were first used
primarily for ornaments and weapons; stone tools were used at
the same time. The early metal tools, made in the image of their
stone predecessors, were thought to possess the same powers
as shaped stone tools, and were called "stones." In some places
metal axes were called "thunderstones," since they were first
made from meteorites which fell from the sky and imitated the
god's act of splitting trees from top to bottom with lightning
bolts. The gestures of the smith forging the tools, and of the
person using the thunderstone, were repetitions of the primor-
dial gesture of the strong god who had flung the stone to
earth. [41] Jesus seems to suggest that the action of using the ax,
itself in the shape of a cross, while re-membering the body, is a
means of experiencing His presence.

Cleave The Wood: I have already spoken of the divinity
within the natural substance, The Wood itself. The heat of my
effort in splitting is used to direct the heat concentrated in the
ax to prepare The Wood for its burning. When the billet is split
in two, the exposed fibers are faces seen for the first time, and
we have the opportunity to encounter the power of the released
Other in its first flush. As the inner flesh of wood is revealed, so
the inner side of the woodsplitter is revealed. By entering the
center of the round whole of the billet, the woodsplitter breaks
it, or, from a psychological point of view, by breaking the
billet, the splitter enters it to discover that "there am I."

The moment I take to be still before the billet, or before the tree, or before the hearth-fire renews these relationships, and has the very practical benefit of calming me before exercise so that my use of my body will be less tense and more effective. If I hear,"No, you may not cut me up," it really does not matter whether I believe that The Wood said this or that I projected my own thought outward into the billet. Either way, there is a tension which will prevent good use of the body. From The Wood's point of view, to effectively remove this tension requires a deeper communication with The Wood, in which a very good reason may be discovered for not cutting or splitting it. From the body's point of view, to effectively remove this tension requires not a domineering inner command but rather a greater stillness, better poise. Emphasis on hurriedly "getting the wood in" can promote a blankness of mind and a misuse of the body, The Wood's revenge. With right use of the body, with supple and erect spine, the stored heat of the ax combines with the heat of my breath to release the sun's energy in The Wood, an awesome consummation in which it has been my privilege to partake.

Notes

1. *Why Split Wood?*

1. *Hesiod, The Homeric Hymns and Homerica,* page 473.

2. The newsletter of the Volunteers in Technical Assistance (3706 Rhode Island Avenue, Mount Ranier, Maryland) for July 1980 reports that among the Sahel of Africa each trip for firewood takes over half a day. Erik Eckholm (*The Other Energy Crisis: Firewood)* reveals how fortunate are those with wood to burn, although in another paper from the Worldwatch Institute, Nigel Smith (*Wood: An Ancient Fuel with a New Future)* is very enthusiastic about increased use of wood for energy. Smith recognizes the obvious fact that some parts of the globe are much better endowed with fuelwood than others. The United States will harvest two *quadrillion* British thermal units (BTUs) this year from the burning of wood, an energy contribution almost as great as nuclear power and growing faster (Lynn Palmer et al., *Wood and Energy).*

3. From the American Heritage Dictionary, also used as the source for many of the etymological references.

4. William Austin, "A Meditation for Christmas-Day," page 36.

5. George Anson, *A Voyage Around the World* .

6. Rudolf Steiner, *Warmth Course,* page 58.

7. John Wallace, *Conversations with Zackary Adams,* page 42.

8. Association of Forest Engineers, "Studies . . ."; H. O. Cook, "Measurement of Fuel Wood"; Reginald Forbes, *Forestry Handbook,* pages 1-48; R. S. Kellogg, "What is a Cord?" A series of reader's letters in *Country Journal,* beginning in November, 1978, has shown a lively debate about what sort of mathematical model is most appropriate for judging the solid wood content of different stacking patterns. Actual field measurements yield more practical information.

9. Karl Gayer, *Forest Utilization,* pages 261-262.

2. *The Tools to Use*

1. Jean Jacques Rousseau, "On the Origin of Inequality," page 335. Though this translation uses the spelling "axe," I shall follow the strong urging of the Oxford English Dictionary to spell the word "ax." "The spelling *ax* is better on every ground, of etymology [Old English, *aex*], phonology [*axe* should be pronounced like *aches*], and analogy [compare with tax and lax]."

2. A. P. and T. E. Penard, "Popular Notions"; George MacCurdy, "The Cult of the Ax"; Mircea Eliade, *The Forge and the Crucible;* Uno Holmberg, *Finno-Ugric Mythology.* Jim Bowie's knife was reputedly made of meteoric stone.

3. Carl Russel, *Firearms, Traps, and Tools,* page 217; Abby Hemenway, *Abby Hemenway's Vermont,* page 13. Notice the use of the word "chip" to mean a chunk or billet.

4. This comparison of output was reported in Brooke Hindle's "Introduction," page 6, and Charles Carroll's "Forest Society of New England," page 19. Other valuable refer-

ences on the ax are Henry Kauffman's *American Axes,* R. A. Salaman's *Dictionary of Tools,* Eric Sloane's *Museum of Early American Tools,* and Alex Bealer's *Old Ways of Working Wood.* The American Axe & Tool Co. *Catalogue* shows the different patterns of blade—Michigan, Kentucky, Adirondack, etc.—whose comparative virtues were once much discussed, but which seem fairly similar to the modern user. Disagreements among these sources as to designs and origins is made more frustrating by their lack of anthroplogical perspective. Petrie's *Tools and Weapons* shows a terrific variety of axes from many different cultures and many periods of history.

5. Reported in Axel Steensberg's *New Guinea Gardens.*

6. There are many variations in technique depending on the constitution of the metal, the purpose of the tool, and the tradition of manufacture. The process is not new: a drop forge identical to this one is described in Sir Francis Head's *A Faggot of French Sticks; or, Paris in 1851.*

7. Mircea Eliade, *The Forge and the Crucible;* Cyril Smith, "The Discovery of Carbon in Steel."

8. Quoted in Stephen Ballew, *et al.,* "Suthin'," pages 44–45.

9. Rudolfs Drillis *et al.,* "The Theory of Striking Tools," and Drillis, "Folk Norms."

10. G. E. Gordon, *Structures,* page 90.

11. These are international specifications from William Armstrong's *Better Tools for the Job,* page 38. A jig similar to this one is used to bend straight helves which have warped.

12. For example, Roger Mitchell's *George Knox.*

13. A screw wedge similar to this one powered by turning a handcrank was mentioned in Gayer's text of 1894, and not recommended.

14. Steensberg, *New Guinea Gardens,* chapter 1.

15. For those familiar with statistics, the error mean square of the analysis of variance was 4.29. The Replications factor gave F (2/6) of 38.79, quite different from random ($p<.01$) as expected. The Treatments factor was also significant ($F(3,6) = 5.28$, $p<.05$). Specific comparisons were as reported, significant differences at least at the .05 level.

16. Eric Jaxheimer, *et al.,* "Woodsplitter Injuries of the Hand," page 87.

17. Ralph Paffenbarger, Jr., *et al.,* "Physical Activity as an Index of Heart Attack Risk"; Ralph Paffenbarger, Jr., and Wayne Hale, "Work Activity and Coronary Heart Mortality."

18. John Nicholson, *The Farmer's Assistant;* Nelson Brown, *Forest Products;* Edwin Betts, *Thomas Jefferson's Farm Book.* The cost recorded in Jamaica, Vermont, in 1812 was $.64 per cord of wood "fit for the fire."

19. E. R. Tichauer and Howard Gage, *Ergonomic Principles.*

20. Thomas Sebeok, *Studies in Cheremis Folklore,* 1.9.1.

21. I also noted that a wood-and-steel wedge was featured in John Alexander's recent book *Make a Chair from a Tree,* as well as in *Early American Tools* by Marshall Davidson and Hans Namuth. All these wedges are mentioned in passing as "modern" in Henry Mercer's *Ancient Carpenters' Tools.*

22. Uno Holmberg, *Finno-Ugric and Siberian Mythology,* page 450.

23. From Accession No. 361, page 13, Northeast Folklore Archives, University of Maine at Orono. Collected by Doris Stackpole in the spring of 1962 from Peter Augustine, a Micmac Indian from Big Cove, New Brunswick, who was working at a farm in Bridgewater, Maine.

24. K. S. Woods, *Rural Crafts of England,* page 197. Introductions to the application of the felling ax can be found in Dudley Cook's *Keeping Warm* and Maurice Cohen's *Woodcutter's Companion,* to the use and care of the crosscut saw in Aldren Watson's "The Cross-Cut Saw" and Warren Miller's *Crosscut Saw Manual.* The best way to learn may be

at one of the many summer and fall woodsmen's contests around the world, three of the biggest being at Hayward, Wisconsin, Boonville, New York, and Albany, Oregon. The only splitting contest which is organized as described earlier is the Labor Day Fair in Guilford, Vermont.

25. Ken Kesey, *Sometimes a Great Notion,* page 197.

26. John Bryan, "The Fire Hazard."

27. Vincent Panella ("The Wood Game") has expressed the woes of many in telling how he split open his finger in the making of kindling.

28. Rudolf Hommel, *China at Work.*

3. *Where and When to Split*

1. Chuang Chou in E. R. Hughes, *Chinese Philosophy,* page 184.

2. Larry Diamond, "Splitting Wood by Hand," page 84.

3. George Tsoumis, *Wood as Raw Material,* pages 50–54. Ratios of tangential to radial shrinkage, a measure of proneness to checking, are given in Bruce Hoadley's *Understanding Wood,* page 74.

4. Heinz Butin and Alex Shigo, *Radial Shakes and "Frost Cracks."*

5. Tom Gajda ("The Effect of Species, Length, and Splitting") measured the moisture content of every inch of an unsplit, partially seasoned white birch log. The moisture content of the outer few inches was fifteen percent, but this increased to fifty percent at the center, too wet for efficient burning.

6. For the statistically oriented, the mean square for error in the analysis of variance was 14.39 (df = 49), and the temperature-knottiness interaction gave an F of 4.89 ($df = 1/49$, $p < .05$). After setting up this comparison, I discovered the generalization that "the softwoods—Aspen, Poplar, Alder, and Sallow—are harder to split when moist than dry, while nearly all the hardwoods are more difficult to split when dry than when green" (John Nisbet, *The Forester,* volume 2, page 449). I only tested hardwoods in this comparison, and found the latter part of the generalization not true, but cannot comment on how moisture affects the splitting of softwoods.

7. Jay Shelton, *Wood Heat Safety;* Jay Shelton *et al.,* "Wood Stove Testing Methods."

8. Thomas Gajda, "The Effect of Species, Length, and Splitting." Figure 16 was compiled from his original data, which he kindly shared with me.

9. Christen Skaar, *Water in Wood.*

10. This assumes that water travels along the grain fifteen times faster than across it, an assumption confirmed by my analysis of Gajda's data.

11. Jay Shelton has written that he now uses a moist-wood basis, that is, the denominator is the original weight. Most texts still prefer a dry-wood basis, as reported here.

12. Cited in Larry Gay's *Heating with Wood,* page 42. The variant given in Robert Graves' *The White Goddess,* page 169, has been put to song by Molly Scott (from the album "Honor the Earth," Sumitra Music, Charlemont, Massachusetts).

13. Jay Shelton, *The Woodburners' Encyclopedia.* Extremely resinous woods give less heat per pound. An interesting comparison is the number of British Thermal Units (BTU's) burned by a human being. A person consuming 3,000 calories each day emits 12,000 BTU's in that time, or less than the burning of 1½ pounds of dry wood.

14. A repeated measures analysis of variance gave an effect size (f) for splitting of .27 and for cutting to a shorter length of .39 ("medium" to "large" effects, according to Jacob Cohen, *Statistical Power Analysis*).

15. Some of these factors are presented in *North Carolina Folklore* (Newman White, editor).

16. Hoadley, *Understanding Wood,* page 111; Samuel Record, *Mechanical Propertie of Wood,* page 42.

4. *Poise and Splitting Firewood*

1. P'ang-yun, *Chu'an Teng Lu,* 8, cited in Alan Watts, *The Way of Zen.*

2. Much more about poise and Alexander's ideas can be found in the books by Edward Maisel and Frank Pierce Jones, as well as in my *Scythe Book.*

3. Raymond A. Dart, "The Attainment of Poise."

4. Roland Gray, *Songs and Ballads,* pages 10–14.

5. I measured several fifths of a cord of green wood and found the average weight to be 963 pounds, or 4,815 pounds per cord. I was interested to find a measurement taken in 1677, from Andrew Yarranton's *England's Improvement by Sea and Land* (page 61): "A Tun and three-quarters of Timber will but make one Coard of Wood." The English tun is 2,240 pounds, leaving Yarranton's cord at 3,920 pounds—either drier or composed of lighter species than my own cords.

6. Alan Watts, *The Way of Zen,* page 133.

7. Miyamoto Musashi, *A Book of Five Rings.* Pictures of sword technique can be found in Morihiro Saito's *Aikido.*

8. Based on the studies by Rudolfs Drillis ("Folk Norms," page 431) among Latvian woodsmen in the 1930's.

9. From the "unwritten sayings of Jesus," presented by Bernard Grenfell and Arthur S. Hunt, *The Oxyrhynchus Papyri,* page 3. Compare with Jacob Bronowski's regard for "the splitting of wood or stone; for by that action the hand (armed with a tool) probes and explores beneath the surface, and thereby becomes an instrument of discovery" (*The Ascent of Man, page 94*).

10. From *The Rambler,* 1752, page 85, cited in W. Jackson Bate's *Samuel Johnson,* page 118.

11. Dudley Cook, *Keeping Warm,* page 67.

12. Arun Garg, "What Criteria Exist for Determining How Much Load Can Be Lifted Safely?"; American Industrial Hygiene Association, *Ergonomics Guide to Manual Lifting.*

13. To sort out Peavey, cant-hook, and cant-dog, I travelled to Bangor, Maine, "Lumber Capital of the World" (in the late 1800's) where the Peavey Co. still exists, and to the Northeast Archives of Folklore and Oral History in nearby Orono, to speak with its director, Edward Ives. I doubt that this will decrease the fervor of this favorite lunchtime discussion among woodsmen.

14. Benjamin Pang Jeng Lo, *The Essence of T'ai Chi Ch'uan,* page 21.

5. *The Wood*

1. Bruno Bettelheim, *The Uses of Enchantment,* page 93.

2. *The Findhorn Garden,* by the Findhorn Community, is an excellent expression of this approach, though many individuals and communities can be found pursuing this same intimacy with nature spirits.

3. Mircea Eliade, *Myth of the Eternal Return.*

4. Sign on a tree in a park in Madrid, quoted by Helen Nearing, *Wise Words,* page 87.

5. A partial list from Maurice Ravel's "Ronde, Trois Chansons," written in 1916.

6. We consume more weight of wood, from cradles to coffins, than the combined weight of all other substances, about one ton per person per year (Bruce Hoadley, *Understanding Wood*, page 230).

7. E. R. Hughes, *Chinese Philosophy*, pages 216f.

8. C. G. Jung, *Collected Works*, volume 5, *passim*.

9. C. G. Jung, *Collected Works*, volume 5, par. 367.

10. Jane Vessels, "Fàtima: Beacon for Portugal's Faithful," page 833.

11. Hugo Rahner, "The Christian Mystery."

12. Chuang Chou, third century B.C., in E. R. Hughes, *Chinese Philosophy*, page 171.

13. Saying of the Cheremiss people, from Uno Holmberg, *Finno–Ugric and Siberian Mythology*, page 235.

14. E. Washburn Hopkins, *Origin and Evolution of Religion*, page 50.

15. *Consumer Reports*, January 1981.

16. John Ott, *Health and Light;* a great variety of research reports are collected in Luke Thorington's *Biologic Aspects of Environmental Lighting*.

17. C. M. Edsman, cited in Mircea Eliade, "Experiences of the Mystic Light," page 61.

18. Stephanie Demetrakopoulos, "Hestia, Goddess of the Hearth"; Claude Levi-Strauss, *The Raw and the Cooked*.

19. Levi-Strauss, *ibid.*

20. Uno Holmberg, *op. cit.,* page 452.

21. This accident is pictured very well in the film *Sometimes a Great Notion*. Other stories about the "barber's chair" are in Dudley Cook's *Keeping Warm*.

22. Eric Jaxheimer, *et al.*, "Woodsplitter Injuries of the Hand."

23. From a letter by the painter Thomas Cole in 1836, cited in Barbara Novak's *Nature and Culture*, page 164. Quite similar in intent is W. H. Auden's more recent "Woods," in *The Shield of Achilles*, and John Fowles' *The Tree*. Martin Buber's passage beginning, "I contemplate a tree," is especially moving, and implies the same threat for not relating (*I and Thou*, pages 57–59).

24. Russell Lockhart, "Cancer in Myth and Dream," from which this story is taken, pages 17–18, originally from Dawkins' *Stories*. Ovid's story of Erysichthon (Book 8) is also graphically expressive, as is the plight of Fradubio in Spencer's *Faerie Queene*. One can easily read the original *Pinocchio*, by Collodi, as the tail end of the same predicament: a rascal has gotten stuck in the wood and must learn many lessons before getting out again.

25. Three books, each titled *Paul Bunyan*, by James Stevens, Esther Shephard, and Wallace Wadsworth. Paul's "life-size" statue rises thirty-one feet in Bangor, Maine, with a double-bitted ax and a cant–dog nearly as tall, but his actual size varies from story to story depending on his feats.

26. R. Vaughan Williams and A. L. Lloyd, *English Folk Songs*, pages 56–57.

27. Mircea Eliade, "Ropes and Puppets," page 165.

28. From the *Bereshit rabba*, cited in Mircea Eliade, "Mephistopheles and the Androgyne," page 104.

29. C. G. Jung, *Collected Works*, especially volumes 5, 12, 13, and 14.

30. Mircea Eliade, *Myth of the Eternal Return*, and "Methistopheles and the Androgyne"; Marie-Louise von Franz, *Creation Myths*, Chapter 9.

31. Last two lines of "Crazy Jane Talks with the Bishop," written in 1933 by W. B. Yeats, *Collected Poems*, page 255.

32. Good examples can be found in Franz Boas, "Tsimshian Mythology," pages 800–803, also Leo Frachtenberg, *Alsea Texts*, pages 119–121.

33. John Layard, *Stone Men of Malekula*.

34. Uno Holmberg, *op. cit.,* pages 252–253.

35. Ovid, *Metamorphoses,* Book 10, especially lines 480–518.

36. Sidney Hartland, "Cleft Ashes"; George Lyman Kittredge, *Witchcraft,* page 148.

37. Franz Boas, "Tsimshian Mythology," page 802.

38. Harold Thompson, *Body, Boots and Britches,* page 51; Mildred Larson, "Lore from Snow Country," pages 265–266; Richard Dorson "Comic Indian Anecdotes," page 122; Emelyn Gardner, *Folklore from the Schoharie Valley,* pages 26–27; Northeast Archives of Folklore and Oral History (University of Maine at Orono), Accession no. 463.

39. Bernard Grenfell and Arthur S. Hunt, *The Oxyrhynchus Papyri,* page 3. The more recent discovery of a more complete Coptic translation of the early Greek texts shows them to be part of the Gnostic Gospel of Thomas (Robert Grant, *The Secret Sayings of Jesus*).

40. Marie-Louise von Franz, *Number and Time.*

41. Mircea Eliade, *Forge and the Crucible.*

References

Alexander, John D. *Make a Chair from a Tree: An Introduction to Working Green Wood*. Newtown, CT: The Taunton Press, 1978.

American Axe and Tool Co. *Illustrated Catalogue*. Columbia, MO: Mid-West Tool Collectors Association, 1981 (1894).

American Industrial Hygiene Association. *Ergonomics Guide to Assessment of Metabolic and Cardiac Costs of Physical Work*. Akron, OH: American Industrial Hygiene Association, 1971.

American Industrial Hygiene Association. *Ergonomics Guide to Manual Lifting*. Akron, OH: American Industrial Hygiene Association, 1970.

Anson, George. *A Voyage around the World*. London: John Knapton, 1748.

Armstrong, William. *Better Tools for the Job*. London: Intermediate Technology Publications, 1980.

Association of Forest Engineers for the Province of Quebec. Studies of the Board Foot, Cubic Foot, and Cord Units of Wood Measurement. *Journal of Forestry*, 1928, *26:*7, 913–928.

Auden, W. H. Woods, *The Shield of Achilles*. New York: Random House, 1951.

Austin, William. A Meditation for Christmas-Day, *Devotionis Augustinianae Flamma, or, Certaine Devout, Godly, and Learned Meditations*. London: J. L. and Ralph Mab, 1635 (1622).

Ballew, Stephen, Joan Brooks, Dona Brotz, and Edward Ives. "Suthin" (It's the Opposite of Nothin'): An Oral History of Grover Morrison's Woods Operation at Little Musquash Lake, 1945–1947. *Northeast Folklore*, 1977, *18* (entire volume).

Bate, W. Jackson. *Samuel Johnson*. New York: Harcourt Brace Jovanovich, 1975.

Bealer, Alex. *Old Ways of Working Wood*. Barre, MA: Barre Publication Co., 1980.

Bettelheim, Bruno. *The Uses of Enchantment*. New York: Knopf, 1976.

Betts, Edwin (Ed.). *Thomas Jefferson's Farm Book*. Princeton, NJ: Princeton University Press, 1953.

Boas, Franz. Tsimshian Mythology. *Annual Report of the Bureau of American Ethnology*, 1909, *31*, 29–1037.

Bronowski, Jacob. *The Ascent of Man*. Boston: Little Brown, 1973.

Brown, Nelson C. *Forest Products.* New York: John Wiley, 1927.

Bryan, John. The Fire Hazard. *Wood,* 1943, *8,* 260–262.

Buber, Martin. *I and Thou* (Walter Kaufmann, trans.). New York: Charles Scribner's Sons, 1970 (1937).

Butin, Heinz, and Alex L. Shigo. *Radial Shakes and "Frost Cracks" in Living Oak Trees* (Forest Service Research Paper NE-478). Washington, DC: United States Department of Agriculture, 1981.

Carroll, Charles F. The Forest Society of New England. In Brooke Hindle (Ed.). *America's Wooden Age.* Tarrytown, NY: Sleepy Hollow Restorations, 1975, 13–36.

Cohen, Jacob. *Statistical Power Analysis.* New York: Academic Press, 1969.

Cohen, Maurice. *The Woodcutter's Companion.* Emmaus, PA: Rodale Press, 1981.

Collodi, C. *The Adventures of Pinocchio* (Carol Della Chiesa, Trans.). New York: Macmillan, 1969 (1883).

Cook, D. *Keeping Warm with an Ax.* New York: Universe Books, 1981.

Cook, H. O. Measurement of Fuel Wood. *Journal of Forestry,* 1918, *16,* 920–921.

Coté, Wilfred A., Jr. (Ed.) *Cellular Ultrastructure of Woody Plants.* Syracuse: Syracuse University Press, 1965.

Dart, Raymond A. The Attainment of Poise. *South African Medical Journal,* 1947, *21,* 74–91 (also *Human Potential,* 1968, *1*).

Davidson, Marshall B., and Hans Namuth. *Early American Tools.* Verona, Italy: Olivetti, 1975.

Dawkins, R. M. *Forty-Five Stories from the Dodekanese.* Cambridge: Cambridge University Press, 1950.

Demetrakopoulos, Stephanie A. Hestia, Goddess of the Hearth: Notes on an Oppressed Archetype. *Spring: An Annual of Archetypal Psychology and Jungian Thought,* 1979, 55–75.

Diamond, Larry. Splitting Wood by Hand. *Organic Gardening and Farming,* November 1978, 84–92.

Dorson, Richard. Comic Indian Anecdotes. *Southern Folklore Quarterly,* 1946, *10,* 122.

Douglass, William. *A Summary, Historical and Political, of the First Planting, Progressive Improvements, and Present State of the British Settlement in North-America,* 2 volumes. Boston: Daniel Fowle, 1749–1751.

Drillis, Rudolfs J. Folk Norms and Biomechanics. *Human Factors,* 1963, *5,* 427–441.

Drillis, Rudolfs, Daniel Schneck, and Howard Gage. The Theory of Striking Tools. *Human Factors,* 1963, *5,* 467–478.

Eckholm, Erik. *The Other Energy Crisis: Firewood* (Worldwatch Paper 1). Washington, DC: Worldwatch Institute, 1975.

Eliade, Mircea. Experiences of the Mystic Light, *The Two and the One* (J. M. Cohen, trans.). Chicago: University of Chicago Press, 1965 (1959), 19–77.

Eliade, Mircea. Mephistopheles and the Androgyne, or the Mystery of the Whole, *The Two and the One* (J. M. Cohen, trans.). Chicago: University of Chicago Press, 1965 (1958), 78–124.

Eliade, Mircea. Ropes and Puppets, *The Two and the One* (J. M. Cohen, trans.). Chicago: University of Chicago Press, 1965 (1961).

Eliade, Mircea. *The Forge and the Crucible* (Stephen Corrin, trans.). New York: Harper & Row, 1962.

Eliade, Mircea. *The Myth of the Eternal Return, or, Cosmos and History* (Willard Trask, trans.). Princeton, NJ: Princeton University Press, 1974 (1949).

Farnsworth, Charles H., and Cecil J. Sharp (Eds.) *Folk-Songs, Chanteys and Singing Games*. New York: H. W. Gray Co., n.d.

Findhorn Community. *The Findhorn Garden*. New York: Harper and Row, 1975.

Flanders, Helen Hartness, Elizabeth Flanders Ballard, George Brown, and Phillips Barry (Eds.). *The New Green Mountain Songster*. Hatboro, PA: Folklore Associates, 1966 (1939).

Forbes, Reginald. *Forestry Handbook*. New York: Ronald Press, 1955.

Fowles, John, with Frank Horvat. *The Tree*. Boston: Little Brown and Co., 1979.

Frachtenberg, Leo J. *Alsea Texts and Myths* (Bulletin 67, Bureau of American Ethnology). Washington, DC: Government Printing Office, 1920.

Franz, Marie-Louise von. *Number and Time* (Andrea Dykes, trans.). Evanston, IL: Northwestern University Press, 1979.

Franz, Marie-Louise von. *Patterns of Creativity Mirrored in Creation Myths*. Zurich: Spring Publications, 1972.

Frazer, Sir James George. *The Golden Bough* (3rd ed.), thirteen volumes. New York: Macmillan, 1966 (1911).

Frazer, Sir James George. *The Magic Art* (volume 4 of *The Golden Bough*, 3rd ed.). New York: Macmillan, 1966 (1911).

Gajda, Thomas Paul. The effect of species, length, and splitting on the drying time of firewood. Unpublished senior thesis, University of Massachusetts at Amherst, 1978.

Gardner, Emelyn. *Folklore from Schoharie Valley*. Ann Arbor: University of Michigan Press, 1937.

Garg, Arun, and M. M. Ayoub. What Criteria Exist for Determining How

Much Load Can Be Lifted Safely? *Human Factors,* 1980, *22,* 475–486.

Gay, Larry. *Heating with Wood.* Charlotte, VT: Garden Way Publishing, 1974.

Gayer, Karl. *Forest Utilization* (W. R. Fisher, trans. volume 5 of *Schlich's Manual of Forestry,* 2nd ed.). London: Bradbury, Agnew and Co., 1908 (1894).

Gordon, T. E. *Structures.* New York: Plenum, 1978.

Grant, Robert M. *The Secret Sayings of Jesus.* Garden City, NY: Doubleday, 1960.

Graves, Robest. *The White Goddess: A Historical Grammar of Poetic Myth* (Enlarged edition). New York: Farrar, Straus and Giroux, 1948.

Gray, Roland P. *Songs and Ballads of the Maine Lumberjacks.* Cambridge, MA: Harvard University Press, 1924.

Grenfell, Bernard, and Arthur S. Hunt (Eds.). *The Oxyrhynchus Papyri,* Part 1. London: Graeco–Roman Branch, Egypt Exploration fund, 1898.

Hartland, E. Sidney. Cleft Ashes for Infantile Hernia. *Folk-Lore,* 1896, *7,* 303–306.

Head, Sir Franicis. *A Faggot of French Sticks; or, Paris in 1851.* New York: George Putnam, 1852.

Hemenway, Abby Maria. *Abby Hemenway's Vermont.* Brattleboro, VT: Stephen Greene Press, 1972.

Hesiod, the Homeric Hymns and Homerica (Hugh G. Evelyn-White, trans.). London: William Heinemann, 1920.

Hindle, Brooke. Introduction: The Span of the Wooden Age. In Brooke Hindle (Ed.) *America's Wooden Age.* Tarrytown, NY: Sleepy Hollow Restorations, 1975, 3–12.

Hoadley, R. Bruce. *Understanding Wood: A Craftsman's Guide to Wood Technology.* Newtown, CT: The Taunton Press, 1980.

Holmberg, Uno. *Finno-Ugric and Siberian Mythology* (Volume 4 of *The Mythology of All Races,* J. A. MacCulloch, ed.). New York: Cooper Square Publishers, 1964 (1932).

Hommel, Rudolf. *China at Work.* New York: John Day, 1937.

Hopfen, H. J., and E. Biesalski. *Small Farm Implements* (Development Paper No. 32). Rome: Food and Agriculture Organization of the United Nations, 1953.

Hopkins, E. Washburn. *Origin and Evolution of Religion.* New Haven: Yale University Press, 1923.

Hughes, E. R. (Ed.) *Chinese Philosophy in Classical Times.* London: J. M. Dent & Sons, 1942.

Jaxheimer, Eric C., William D. Morain, and Forest E. Brown. Woodsplitter Injuries of the Hand. *Plastic and Reconstructive Surgery,* July 1981, 83–88.

Jennings, Neal E., and Gary G. Naughton. *Firewood Plantations.* Manhattan, KS: Cooperative Extension Service, Kansas State University, 1979.

Johnson, Samuel. *The Rambler* (W. J. Bate and Albrecht Strauss, eds.). New Haven: Yale University Press, 1969 (1750–1752).

Jones, Frank Pierce. *Body Awareness in Action: A Study of the Alexander Technique.* New York: Schocken Books, 1976.

Jung, C. G. *Collected Works* (Bollingen Series XX). Princeton: Princeton University Press, 1968.

Kauffman, Henry J. *American Axes: A Survey of Their Development and their Makers.* Brattleboro, VT: Stephen Greene Press, 1972.

Kellogg, R. S. What is a Cord? *Journal of Forestry,* 1925, *23,* 608–610.

Kesey, Ken. *Sometimes a Great Notion.* New York: Viking Press, 1964.

Kittredge, George Lyman. *Witchcraft in Old and New England.* Cambridge: Harvard University Press, 1929.

Langsner, Drew. *Country Woodcraft.* Emmaus, PA: Rodale Press, 1978.

Larson, Mildred. Lore from Snow Country. *New York Folklore Quarterly,* 1955, *11,* 262–274.

Layard, John. *Stone Men of Malekula.* London: Chatto & Windus, 1942.

Levi-Strauss, Claude. *The Raw and the Cooked: Introduction to a Science of Mythology: 1* (John and Doreen Weightman, trans.). New York: Harper & Row, 1975 (1964).

Lockhart, Russell. Cancer in Myth and Dream: An Exploration into the Archetypal Relation Between Dreams and Disease. *Spring,* 1977, 1–26.

MacCurdy, George Grant. The Cult of the Ax. In F. W. Hodge (Ed.) *Holmes Anniversary Volume: Anthropological Essays Presented to William Henry Holmes.* Washington: private edition, 1916, 301–315.

MacDonald, George. *Phantastes and Lilith.* Grand Rapids, Michigan: William Eerdmans Publishing Company, 1964 (1858, 1895).

Maisel, Edward. *The Resurrection of the Body: The Writings of F. Matthias Alexander.* New York: Delta, 1969.

Mercer, Henry C. *Ancient Carpenters' Tools: Together with Lumberman's, Joiners', and Cabinet Makers' Tools in Use in the Eighteenth Century,* 5thed. Doyleston, PA: Bucks County Historical Society, 1975 (1929).

Miller, Warren. *Crosscut Saw Manual.* Washington, DC: Forest Service, United States Department of Agriculture, 1978.

Mitchell, Roger E. George Knox: From Man to Legend. *Northeast Folklore,* 1969, *11* (entire volume).

Musashi, Miyamoto. *A Book of Five Rings* (Victor Harris, trans.). London: Allison and Busby, 1974 (1645).

Nearing, Helen. *Wise Words on the Good Life.* New York: Schocken Books, 1980.

Needham, Walter, with Barrows Mussey. *A Book of Country Things.* Brattleboro, VT: The Stephen Greene Press, 1965.

Nicholson, John, *The Farmer's Assistant.* Albany: H. C. Southwick, 1815.

Nisbet, John. *The Forester,* volume 2. London: William Blackwood and Sons, 1950.

Novak, Barbara. *Nature and Culture: American Landscape and Painting, 1825–1875.* New York: Oxford University Press, 1980.

Ott, John. *Health and Light.* Old Greenwich, CT: Devin–Adair Company, 1973.

Ovid (Publius Ovidius Naso). *Metamorphoses* (Rolfe Humphries, trans.). Bloomington: Indiana University Press, 1955 (first century A.D.).

Paffenbarger, Ralph S., Jr., and Wayne Hale. Work Activity and Coronary Heart Mortality. *New England Journal of Medicine,* 1975, *292,* 545–550.

Paffenbarger, Ralph S., Jr., Alvin Wing, and Robert Hyde. Physical Activity as an Index of Heart Attack Risk in College Alumni. *American Journal of Epidemiology,* 1978, *108,* 161–175.

Palmer, Lynn, Robert McKusick, and Mark Bailey. *Wood and Energy in New England.* Washington, DC: Natural Resource Economics Division of the Economics, Statistics, and Cooperatives Service of the United States Department of Agriculture, 1980.

Panella, Vincent. The Wood Game. *Country Journal,* April 1979, p. 93.

Pang Jeng Lo, Benjamin, Martin Inn, Robert Amacker, and Susan Foe (Eds.). *The Essence of T'ai Chi Ch'uan.* Richmond, CA: North Atlantic Books, 1979.

Penard, A. P., and T. E. Popular Notions Pertaining to Primitive Stone Artifacts. *Journal of American Folklore,* 1917, *30,* 251–261.

Perrin, Noel. Foolproof Wood Splitting. *UpCountry,* December 1979, 10–11.

Petrie, William. History in Tools. *Annual Report, Smithsonian Institute.* Washington, DC: Smithsonian Institute, 1920 (1917), 563–572.

Petrie, William. *Tools and Weapons.* London: British School of Archaeology in Egypt, 1917.

Rahner, Hugo. The Christian Mystery and the Pagan Mysteries. In Joseph Campbell (Ed.) *The Mysteries* (Bollingen Series XXX, 2). Princeton: Princeton University Press, 1955 (1944), 337–401.

Record, Samuel J. *The Mechanical Properties of Wood.* New York: John Wiley, 1914.

Regional Self-Reliance Project. *Tri-State Region Fuelwood Resources: An Assessment.* Keene, NH: Antioch/New England Graduate School, 1980.

Rousseau, Jean Jacques. On the Origin of Inequality (G.D.H. Cole, trans.). In Robert Hutchins (Ed.). *Great Books of the Western World,* volume 38. Chicago: Encyclopedia Brittanica, 1952 (1755).

Rowsome, Frank, Jr. *The Bright and Glowing Place.* Brattleboro, VT: Stephen Greene Press, 1975.

Russell, Carl P. *Firearms, Traps, and Tools of the Mountain Men.* New York: Knopf, 1967.

Saito, Morihiro. *Aikido.* Tokyo: Minato Research and Publishing Co., 1973.

Salaman, R. A. *Dictionary of Tools, Used in the Woodworking and Allied Trades, c. 1700–1970.* London: George Allen & Unwin, 1975.

Sandburg, Carl. *Abraham Lincoln: The Prairie Years.* New York: Harcourt, Brace & Co., 1926.

Sebeok, Thomas A. (Ed.) *Studies in Cheremis Folklore* (Indiana University Folklore Series No. 6). Bloomington: University of Indiana, 1952.

Shelton, Jay W. *Wood Heat Safety.* Charlotte, VT: Garden Way Publishing, 1979.

Shelton, Jay. *The Woodburners' Encyclopedia.* Waitsfield, VT: Vermont Crossroads Press, 1976.

Shelton, J. W., T. Black, M. Chaffee, and M. Schwartz. Wood Stove Testing Methods and Some Preliminary Experimental Results. *American Society of Heating, Refrigeration, and Air-Conditioning Engineers (ASHRAE) Transactions,* 1978, *48,* Part 1, 388–404.

Shephard, Esther. *Paul Bunyan.* New York: Harcourt, Brace & Co., 1952.

Skaar, Christen. *Water in Wood.* Syracuse: University of Syracuse Press, 1972.

Sloane, Eric. *A Museum of Early American Tools.* New York: Funk & Wagnalls, 1964.

Sloane, Eric. *A Reverence for Wood.* New York: Ballantine, 1965.

Smith, Cyril Stanley. The Discovery of Carbon in Steel. *Technology and Culture,* 1964, *5*(2), 149–175.

Smith, Nigel. *Wood: An Ancient Fuel with a New Future* (Worldwatch Paper 42). Washington, DC: Worldwatch Institute, 1981.

Smyser, Steve. When an Axe is Not Enough. In Diana Branch (Ed.). *Tools for Homesteaders, Gardeners, and Small-Scale Farmers.* Emmaus, PA: Rodale Press, 1978, 448–452.

Steensberg, Axel. *New Guinea Gardens: A Study of Husbandry with Parallels in Prehistoric Europe.* New York: Academic Press, 1980.

Steiner, Rudolf. *Warmth Course: The Theory of Heat.* Spring Valley, NY: Mercury Press, 1980 (1920).

Stephens, Rockwell. *Axes & Chainsaws: Use & Maintenance.* Charlotte, VT: Garden Way Associates, 1977.

Stevens, James. *Paul Bunyan.* New York: Alfred Knopf, 1948.

Thomas, J. J. *The Illustrated Annual Register of Rural Affairs and Cultivator Almanac for the year 1873.* Albany, NY: Luther Tucker & Son, 1873.

Thompson, Harold W. *Body, Boots and Britches.* Philadelphia, 1940.

Thoreau, Henry D. *Journal* (Bradford Torrey and Francis H. Allen, eds.). New York: Dover Publications, 1962.

Thoreau, Henry David. *Walden* (Philip Van Doren Stern, ed.). New York: Clarkson N. Potter, 1970 (1854).

Thorington, Luke (Ed.). *Biologic Aspects of Environmental Lighting.* North Bergen, NJ: Duro-Test Corporation, n.d.

Tichauer, E. R., and Gage, Howard. *Ergonomic Principles Basic to Hand Tool Design.* Akron, OH: American Industrial Hygiene Association, 1977.

Tresemer, David. Field Testing the Splitting Tools. *Country Journal,* September 1980, 74–79.

Tresemer, David. *The Scythe Book: Mowing Hay, Cutting Weeds, and Harvesting Small Grains with Hand Tools.* Brattleboro, VT: By Hand & Foot, 1981.

Tsoumis, George. *Wood as Raw Material.* Oxford: Pergamon Press, 1968.

The Use of Wood for Fuel (Bulletin 753). Washington, DC: United States Dept. of Agriculture, 1919.

Vessels, Jane. Fàtima: Beacon for Portugal's Faithful. *National Geographic,* December 1980, 832–839.

Wadsworth, Wallace. *Paul Bunyan and his Great Blue Ox.* Garden City, NY: Doubleday & Co., 1964 (1926).

Wallace, John. *Conversations with Zackary Adams.* Brattleboro, VT: Stephen Daye Press, 1943.

Watson, Aldren A. The Six-foot, Two-man Crosscut. *Country Journal,* March 1980, 53–59.

Watts, Alan. *The Way of Zen.* New York: Vintage, 1957.

White, Newman (Ed.). *North Carolina Folklore,* volume 7. Durham, NC: Duke University Press, 1964.

Williams, R. Vaughan, and A. L. Lloyd (Eds.) *English Folk Songs.* Hammondsworth: Penguin Books, 1959.

Wilson, Ernest H. *Aristocrats of the Trees.* New York: Dover, 1974 (1930).

Wood Fuel in Wartime (Farmer's Bulletin #1912). Washington, DC: United States Dept. of Agriculture, 1942.

Woodberry, George. *A History of Wood-Engraving.* New York: Harper & Brothers, 1883.

Woods, K. S. *Rural Crafts of England.* London: George Harrap and Co., 1949.

Yarranton, Andrew. *England's Improvement by Sea and Land.* London, 1677.

Yeats, W. B. *The Collected Poems.* New York: Macmillan Co., 1933.

Index

141